AN ATTRACTI

Something had happened in Stephen Moore's life that had made him hard and embittered, unable to care for any woman. But that didn't stop Joanna loving him dearly. Would her love ever be strong enough to break the shell he had built around himself?

AN ATTRACTION OF OPPOSITES

BY

SANDRA FIELD

MILLS & BOON LIMITED
15–16 BROOK'S MEWS
LONDON W1A 1DR

First published 1983
Australian copyright 1983
Philippine copyright 1983
This edition 1983

© Sandra Field 1983

ISBN 0 263 74355 1

Set in Monophoto Times 10 on 10½ pt.
01–1083 – 60534

Made and printed in Great Britain by
Richard Clay (The Chaucer Press) Ltd,
Bungay, Suffolk

CHAPTER ONE

THE gusts of chill Atlantic wind carried the haunting call of the geese to the slim, red-haired girl standing so still beside her car. In a ragged V-formation the great birds drifted down to earth, where the stalks of last year's corn stood in neat rows in the field and the last of the winter snow lay unmelted in the furrows: geometric lines of red soil, white snow, red soil, stretching as far as the eye could see. It almost seemed to Joanna that she could hear the beat of air against the many wings as the birds, moving like one, sank lower, then became earthbound, until they were only so many dark specks against the fields.

She had been travelling along the narrow dirt road doing the egg deliveries, concentrating on her driving, for the road was sleek with mud now that spring was finally coming to the Island. Then something had made her look up. The minute she had seen the synchronised beat of wings against the cloudy sky, she had stopped the car and got out. She could not have explained the attraction these wild and beautiful birds had for her. Canada geese—long-necked and majestic, wily and sagacious. As soon as the ice started to melt on the rivers they arrived from the south, great flocks of them blackening the sky. For a month the Island was their home; they gathered in the bays and inlets, feeding in the open meadows. By the middle of May they were gone, flying northward to nest and raise their young. But in the autumn they would return, plump from their summer feeding, to remain until ice again claimed the waterways and the imperative call of the south could no longer be ignored. To Joanna they epitomised the mystery and beauty of nature, of all that was wild and free.

Now she gave a little sigh. She'd better get back to work. Mrs Robertson would be waiting for her weekly delivery of a dozen brown-shelled eggs, and the kettle would be bubbling on the stove. Banging her gloved fingers together, Joanna got back in the car. A cup of tea would hit the spot right now. It was cold, the raw, biting cold of April in Prince Edward Island when the sea ice was still packed against the shoreline and the winds seemed to come straight from the North Pole.

Cautiously she engaged the clutch. John had insisted she bring his car rather than her own; his was considerably older than hers, and needed handling with a carefully tuned mixture of bravado and sensitivity. She picked up speed, avoiding two gaping potholes filled with dirty brown water, and from long experience also avoiding the shoulders of the road where the mud was soft and glutinous and the car could sink axle-deep in no time. Hands firm on the wheel, which reverberated and quivered with a life of its own, she began to hum to herself.

Then everything seemed to happen so quickly that afterwards Joanna had difficulty piecing it together. It was all the fault of the geese, that much was certain. She was only a couple of miles from Mrs Robertson's when something made her look up; over a copse of naked-limbed trees a huge V of birds fanned across the windswept sky. Joanna gazed at them in delight, not even seeing the red-painted Stop sign ahead. They were so incredibly beautiful in their grace and freedom; they made her want to leave her island home, to take wing herself and fly she knew not where. . . .

There was a crash of metal on metal, a splintering of glass. Her head banged against the windshield as the wheel was jolted from her hands. She was not aware of jamming on the brake, but she must have done so at the instant of impact, for the old car had come to a shuddering halt. The world rocked on its axis and Joanna closed her eyes, fighting back a wave of nausea and dizziness.

Her door was jerked open—it had a squeal all of its own which Joanna would have recognised anywhere—and a man's harsh voice demanded, 'Are you all right?'

Her forehead resting on the wheel, she swallowed hard. Then she forced herself to look up. The eyes that met hers were unlike any she had ever seen before: long-lashed and deep-set, they were an opaque shade of grey. But grey was far too ordinary a word, she thought dazedly. They were like rock. Granite. Hard and unyielding. There was a patina of concern over them now, but even confused as she was, she was not deceived by that; for underneath lay anger, all the more frightening for being held back. Impatiently he repeated, 'Are you all right?'

'I—I think so.' She touched her forehead gingerly. 'I must have hit my head.'

'Looks as though it struck the windshield. Here, you'd better get out—let me give you a hand.'

'I can manage.'

But when she had eased herself out of the seat and went to stand up, she discovered that her knees were like jelly and that she was shaking all over. She felt his arms go around her and knew that without them she would have subsided into an ignominious heap on the ground. She rested her cheek against his jacket, breathing shallowly, her eyes closed against a light that suddenly seemed glaringly bright. Briefly time and all the demands of reality were suspended.

Into her consciousness gradually crept a number of impressions. The fabric her cheek was leaning against was suede, smooth and pliable and expensive. Her nose was buried in his sweater; while she had never owned anything so soft and finely woven, she would be willing to bet that it was cashmere—also expensive. Then she became aware of other things: the heavy beat of his heart, slower, far stronger than hers; an indefinably masculine odour, clean yet somehow disturbing, that came from his clothes—and from the body beneath, she thought, with the first touch of unease; a sensation of latent strength from the arms that encircled her and from the hard wall of his chest against which she was leaning. Had been leaning for far too long, she decided in a sudden panic that was as intense as it was irrational.

She pushed herself away from him, again meeting those impenetrable grey eyes. 'I feel better now,' she faltered. 'I—what happened, anyway?'

'What happened is that you drove straight into me,' he replied grimly.

'Oh, no——'

'Oh, yes. Didn't you see the Stop sign?'

Joanna looked around her, seeing for the first time that she was standing at the intersection of two roads, the dirt one on which she had been travelling and a paved one that was the most direct route to John's farm. Because she could no longer avoid doing so, she also looked at the cars. The stranger had struck her right front wheel, crumpling the fender, denting the mudguard, and flattening the tyre. His car, she saw sickly, was a Mercedes, a sleek black station wagon, as expensive and well-bred as its owner. Fortunately it appeared as though John's car had taken the brunt of the collision, although there were two deep scratches in the shiny black paint and the chrome rim around the headlight was bent. She said helplessly, 'I'm sorry. I'll pay for any damage to your car.'

If she had expected gratitude, she was soon disappointed. 'It's easy to say you're sorry,' was the uncompromising reply. 'What I'd like to know is what the devil you were doing that you didn't even slow down for the intersection—I was, as you see, going on the assumption that you would stop.'

Whatever her faults, dishonesty was not among them. 'I wasn't paying attention——' she began.

'Obviously.'

His voice was laden with sarcasm and something in it

caught her on the raw. Her chin tilted defiantly. 'I've said I was sorry and I'll pay for the damage. You don't have to act as if I've committed a murder!'

'If you'd been going much faster, you could have. It borders on the criminal to drive without watching what you're doing.'

That he was absolutely right didn't help matters at all. Hot colour flooded her cheeks. 'I'm damned if I'll apologise again!'

'For a minute I was afraid I might have killed you!'

His furiously spoken statement stopped her in her tracks, and for the first time she noticed the hint of white about his mouth. 'Then I *am* sorry,' she repeated with genuine remorse. 'I'll truly be more careful in the future.'

He seemed to be singularly unimpressed by her pledge, for all he said was, icily, 'At least do me the courtesy of enlightening me as to what world-shaking matter was occupying your attention. Are you in love? Or did you have a fight with your boy-friend?'

'No and no!' Joanna exploded. Then her head suddenly swung to the right and the anger vanished from her eyes. Quite unconscious of what she was doing, she rested her hand on his sleeve. 'Listen——'

Unwillingly he turned his head to follow her gaze. Above the copse of trees, their limbs a black tracery against the clouds, a long skein of geese straggled across the sullen sky, calling back and forth to each other. Then the wings grew still; the birds hovered, gliding downwards and disappearing behind the trees.

As Joanna gave a tiny sigh of repletion, the man's eyes came back to her. Her green jacket had seen better days, her jeans were patched on both knees, her boots had been chosen for serviceability rather than glamour. But it was her face that drew his gaze and held it. Short auburn hair curled around her ears and the nape of her neck, clinging to her exquisitely shaped head. High cheekbones, grey-green eyes, and a dusting of freckles

over a retroussé nose made a face of unusual beauty.
But it had more than beauty, for her features
mirrored her every emotion—a mobile, vibrantly alive
face. Even as he watched, she dragged her attention
away from the sky and back to him. 'It was the
geese, you see—that's why I wasn't paying attention
to the road.'

It was obvious she considered this brief statement
entirely self-explanatory. 'I don't get you,' he said with
rather overdone patience. 'Would you mind explaining
what's so all-absorbing about a few birds?'

Shocked, she exclaimed, 'But they're not ordinary
birds!' Again she gazed out over the meadow, her eyes
shining softly. 'They fly with the wind and the sky is
their home. . . .' She gave herself a little shake, trying to
be more prosaic. 'Many of them nest in the far north,
and they'll fight with the courage of lions for their
young. They mate for life, you know.'

'Unlike the human species.'

Her eyes flew to his face. She had always thought
Drew the best-looking man she had ever seen, but now
she was not so sure. This man did not have the smooth,
classic good looks that were Drew's, for his features
were far more ruggedly hewn, and again that word
granite slipped into her mind. Prominent cheekbones
and a determined chin, a formidably controlled mouth
and those arresting, deep-set eyes . . . what other words
would she use to describe him? Bored, cynical,
disillusioned? Certainly they all came to mind.
Detached? Yes, that as well. But more than that she
sensed an underlying unhappiness, so deeply ingrained
that perhaps he was not even aware of it himself. Which
brought her back to his remark. 'It's nonsense to say
that. I know some very good marriages that have lasted
for years.'

'Do you, now? Then you've been more fortunate
than I.'

The wind tugged at her parka, ruffling her hair. 'I

think this is a very odd conversation, considering the circumstances.'

He was not to be deflected. 'Tell me one more thing—do you get that excited about everything? Or is it only wild geese?'

With a delightful tinge of self-mockery, she said, 'I wish it were. I do have a tendency to go overboard about things, and as a result I quite often get into trouble.' She looked over at the two cars. 'Like now. Oh dear, I wish I'd been watching where I was going. It would have to be John's car, too, not mine, wouldn't it?'

'John?'

Her expressive face clouded and she missed the implicit question as well as his lightning-swift glance downwards at her ring finger, hidden by a woollen glove at least two sizes too big for her. 'Mmm ... he doesn't need anything like this right now.' She gave another sigh. 'Well, I suppose he's used to me getting into scrapes. Perhaps he won't mind too much.'

Pointedly the stranger looked at his watch. 'I think it's time we extricated ourselves from this particular scrape. Tell me where you keep your spare tyre and I'll change it for you—I think the rest of the damage is fairly superficial.'

'The spare tyre needs air in it,' Joanna said weakly. 'I was supposed to get it pumped up this morning, but I thought I'd deliver the eggs first. Oh, lord, I hope they didn't all get broken!'

'The eggs are the least of my worries. Is the tyre in the trunk? We'll drive to the nearest gas station—there's one a couple of miles down the road, isn't there?'

Joanna looked down at her mud-caked boots and over at the gleaming Mercedes. 'Why don't I wait here?'

'It's much too cold. Get in.'

Something in his voice quelled the protest on her tongue. John, she thought with a faint touch of amusement, would have been surprised to see how meekly she climbed into the stranger's car, although she did first bang her boots together to remove the worst of the mud. The interior of the car smelled pleasantly of leather and pipe tobacco. Trying not to shiver, for the wind had chilled her to the bone and her ears were tingling from the cold, she sat in the front seat, watching as the man—she didn't even know his name, she realised—removed her tyre from the trunk, shut it in his own trunk, then carefully backed her car on to the shoulder of the road. He bent to remove the shards of broken glass from the pavement, tossing them into the ditch. As he straightened, it struck her how tall he was, well over six feet, and how well built; every movement had the controlled power of a man at the peak of physical fitness. More than that, he bore an undefinable stamp of sophistication that had little to do with the well-groomed, peat-brown hair, the pigskin gloves, or the silk ascot; it seemed almost inborn, as much a part of him as the piercing grey eyes and the harsh line of mouth. A man of the city, she was sure of that. So what was he doing here?

One thing was certain, she decided ruefully, looking down at her own worn and unbecoming outfit: she would hardly impress him. Apart from the very literal way in which she already had. . . .

He got back in the car, saying tersely as they began to move forward, 'There is a garage a mile or two down the road, isn't there?'

'Yes.' She added hesitantly, 'I hope you weren't in too much of a hurry?'

He shot her a sardonic, sideways glance. 'Belated pangs of conscience? Ah, well . . . one of the reasons I came here was to escape the tyranny of being totally ruled by the clock. Consider this morning your contribution to the cause.'

Joanna could think of no polite reply to this, although several impolite ones came to mind. Her mutinous green eyes belying the sweetness of her voice, she said, 'You haven't even told me your name.'

'Stephen Moore.' Politely, but with no real interest, he added, 'And yours?'

'Joanna Hailey.' She took the plunge, realising full well that if she did not say something the conversation would die on its feet; he was definitely not a man for small talk. 'You're just a visitor here?'

'No.'

The monosyllable hung in the air. Joanna flushed. 'In other words, I should mind my own business.'

'You put it rather crudely, but yes. I value my privacy—another of the reasons I came here.'

Perhaps fortunately, for Joanna's temper was beginning to rise, the garage came into sight on the left-hand side of the road, and Stephen Moore pulled up beside the air hose. 'Stay in the car—this'll only take a minute.'

He wasn't concerned for her comfort, she fumed inwardly, he simply didn't want her company. As he got back in a few minutes later, she said coldly, 'I know the man who runs this garage—he'll go back to the car with me and change the tyre. That way I won't have to bother you any further.'

'I heard the young fellow inside say something about the owner being off on a job. So you'd have to wait.'

'I'm sure my time is less valuable than yours,' she snapped.

'Anyway,' he finished gently, 'the eggs might freeze, and we can't have that, can we?'

'You're a very exasperating man—do you always have an answer for everything?'

For the first time there was a slight gleam of humour in those unrelenting grey eyes. 'And you're a very forthright young woman—do you always go around saying exactly what's on your mind?'

'I hate playing games—so perhaps I do.'

'Then let me be equally forthright and say I would prefer to do your tyre myself and see you safely on your way.'

And out of your life. . . . 'You'll have to give me your address so that I can pay you for the damage to your car.'

Briefly his eyes flickered over her patched and faded jeans. 'That won't be necessary.'

She sat up a little straighter, her hands clenched in her lap, for she had seen that telltale glance. 'Mr Moore, I don't take charity from anyone. Despite the way I'm dressed, I'm perfectly capable of paying for the repairs to your car.'

They were back at the crossroads again and he braked rather more sharply than was necessary. 'Granted that you are, it still won't be necessary. I have considerably more money than I know what to do with, and the amount it will take to fix the car is a drop in the bucket.'

'You're missing the point,' she said with dangerous calm. 'I'm responsible for the damage—therefore I pay for it.'

'I thought it was John's car.'

'So it is. But that doesn't make any difference—I'll still look after it.' Anxiety clouded the clear green eyes. 'He's got enough money problems as it is.'

'All the more reason why I should pay for the damages, then.'

She turned to face him. 'Don't you understand? It's not *right* that you should pay for it. Please . . . you must allow me to. It's the principle of the thing!'

He looked down at her face, where all her passionate conviction was clearly to be read. 'It really matters to you, doesn't it?'

'Of course it does!'

For the first time since their precipitate meeting, he smiled, and his whole face softened and came alive. Joanna had thought him attractive beforehand, but now she found herself strangely breathless. When he reached up a finger and ran it lightly down her cheek, it was a gesture that seemed all the more intimate because of his earlier reserve, and briefly her lashes flickered. He said with unmistakable sincerity, 'That's very nice of you, Joanna Hailey. It's been a long time since I've run across anyone who still believes in principles—too long, I guess. Thank you.' He reached for the doorhandle. 'Now, let's get that tyre changed.'

Still bemused, Joanna got out as well, watching him draw off his gloves and bend to his self-imposed task. He worked swiftly and efficiently, as if it was a job he had done many times before, and as she took the battered hub-cap and then the bolts from him she said jokingly, 'You could be a mechanic yourself.'

Not looking at her, he said abruptly, 'I was, once.'

She heard her unruly tongue say, 'You don't look like someone who was a mechanic.'

'No?' He pulled the rim free and looked at the tyre. 'That's had it, I'm afraid. You'll have to get a new one. I'll put it in the trunk for now.'

Somehow she knew better than to ask any further questions, and in silence she watched as he put on the spare and tightened the bolts, his lean fingers gripping the wheel wrench with a strength that did not surprise her in the least. When he was finished, and the tools were stowed away again, she passed him a piece of rag to wipe his hands. He had been giving the car a very comprehensive once-over and said decisively, 'Get the brakes, the alignment, and the radiator checked when you take it in for repairs.' Almost reluctantly he added, 'Do you have far to go now?'

'Not that far—I live in Huntleigh. I guess I'll go home first before I finish the egg deliveries.'

Because she was staring gloomily at the broken headlight she missed the flicker of consternation that crossed his face. 'That would probably be wise—you should drive it as little as possible until it's fixed,' was all he said.

From far across the field, carried on the cutting edge of the wind, came the derisive honking of the geese. Joanna said crossly, 'It really was their fault.'

'No doubt. Well, goodbye, Joanna Hailey. I must get on my way.'

She held out a gloved hand and felt him perfunctorily press her fingers. Not the hint of a smile softened the granite eyes. It would seem he was going to disappear from her life as precipitately as he had entered it, this mysterious stranger, who looked as if he had just stepped out of a Toronto haberdashers yet could change a tyre with the expertise of a garage hand; who had told her virtually nothing about himself, yet whose cynicism and detachment had become as real to her as the thick dark hair and the beautifully shaped hands. As she stared at him blankly, saying with meaningless politeness, 'Goodbye, Mr Moore,' she was horrified by the intensity of her regret. She would have liked to have seen him again, to have had the chance to try and get behind the barriers he had erected against—against what? Or whom? She had no idea.

'Next time keep your eyes on the road,' was his parting remark. Then he was smoothly reversing the Mercedes and heading back in the direction of the garage. But his destination could be any one of a dozen places, Joanna knew, for the road to Charlottetown crossed this road only three miles away. In a minute or two the black car disappeared around the bend and she was left alone with only the wind-tossed trees and the cold, wet fields for company. And the geese, she thought ruefully, for once finding herself less than interested in them. She'd better get home and break the news to John. . . .

She drove slowly, discovering several new wobbles in the wheel, and forcing herself to concentrate solely on her driving. Fifteen minutes later she reached Huntleigh, a small village nestled around an inlet of the Gulf of St Lawrence, and turned up the driveway of John's house. Seven-year-old Mark came running to meet her, Misty the collie following more sedately on his heels. 'Hi, Jo! Hey——' in awestruck tones, 'what'd you do to the car?'

'I collided with somebody else.' As she climbed out of the car, it suddenly struck her that Stephen Moore had got away without leaving her his address after all—so he would end up paying for the damages to his car, not she. Oh, damn . . . why it should matter so much she didn't know, but matter it did.

'What kind of a car?' Mark was clamouring. By some kind of genetic quirk he had Joanna's red hair rather than John's light brown or Sally's brunette, and he had a full measure of her excitable nature as well.

'A Mercedes.'

It had all the effect she could have desired. 'Wow!' he exclaimed, temporarily speechless.

'Where's your dad?'

'In the house. He's paying the bills.'

Joanna pulled a face. She did pick her times; finances were a touchy subject these days.

As she trudged up the path she gave the old farmhouse an affectionate look. The porch needed re-shingling and the paint was starting to peel, but she loved every inconvenient corner of it, for she had been coming here for years, ever since John had bought it, and it was like a second home to her.

Mark was tugging at her hand. 'Did Mrs Robertson give you any hockey cards? She promised she'd save some for me.'

'I haven't been there yet, love—I'll have to go back in my car.'

'Can I tell Dad what happened?'

'No!' Fortunately it was a word Mark respected, although he did look rather downcast. Slipping out of her boots and hanging up her jacket, Joanna went into the kitchen, where the woodstove radiated a comforting heat, the birch logs snapping cheerfully. John was seated at the pine table, which was covered with ledgers, cheque books, receipts and bills, the latter, Joanna knew, outnumbering the former. He smiled up at her. 'You're home a bit early, aren't you?'

Never one to beat around the bush, she blurted, 'John, I'm terribly sorry, but I had an accident, just a little one, and damaged the front wheel.' She frowned, trying to remember what Stephen Moore had said. 'You have to check the brakes and the radiator and something else. . . .'

'The alignment,' John supplied drily. 'What happened, Sis?'

She plunked herself down in the chair across from him. 'It was all my fault. I was watching the geese and I didn't see the stop sign. So I ran into another car.'

Mark could keep quiet no longer. 'A Mercedes, Dad!'

'You do pick 'em, don't you, Jo? And how did he fare?'

'Better than me. But he wouldn't let me pay for it. I guess he has a lot of money. But still . . . I wish he'd let me.'

'You couldn't have fluttered your eyelashes enough.'

'Don't be silly,' she retorted crossly. 'I don't go around fluttering my eyelashes at complete strangers.'

'You don't have to—one look out of those big green eyes of yours and they usually do anything you want anyway.'

'Well, not this one,' she said with considerable feeling.

'Really? I'd like to meet him—he must be a rare bird.'

Joanna knew she could be honest with John, for despite the twelve-year gap in their ages there was a deep bond of affection between brother and sister. 'He wasn't like anyone I've ever met before.' The green eyes that John had accused her of using so tellingly were lost in thought. 'He was . . . oh, this sounds ridiculous, and it's really none of my business—as he lost no time in telling me—but I couldn't help feeling that despite all his money, something had gone badly wrong in his life. He wasn't happy, I'm sure of it.'

'He seems to have made quite an impression on you.'

With attempted briskness she said, 'Well, whether he

did or he didn't, it doesn't make much difference, because I certainly won't be seeing him again. In the meantime I'd better put the eggs in my car and finish delivering them.'

'No more bird-watching this time—promise?'

'Faithfully!' She gave him a shamefaced grin. 'I *am* sorry, John. It was a stupid thing to do.' She looked at the welter of papers on the table, flicking a bill with her fingernail; it was one of the many from the Montreal hospital. 'I'm supposed to be helping, not hindering. You've got enough on your mind as it is.'

He glowered at the pile of unpaid accounts. 'Yeah.'

Briefly she rested her hand on his, noticing how he had aged in the last six months, the first grey hairs appearing in his light brown curls and new lines furrowing his forehead. If she was any use at all, she'd put her charms to work and marry a rich man— someone like Stephen Moore, she thought, with a wry twist of her lips. It still rankled that he had so ruthlessly removed himself from any further contact with her. Perhaps John was right. Perhaps she was used to a fair bit of male attention, even took it for granted, so that Stephen Moore's aloofness was all the harder to take. It wasn't a picture of herself that she liked very much.

Resolutely she pushed back her chair. 'I'll be back in an hour to get some lunch.'

'Okay. I'll run the car into the barn—probably I can do a fair bit of the work myself. It's still too wet to plough.'

Joanna's second round of deliveries went smoothly, and she was soon back at the farmhouse, preparing and eating lunch, then clearing away the dishes with the help of Brian, John's elder son. He was a ten-year-old replica of his father in looks and temperament, for he was as quiet and easygoing as Mark was exuberant. Afterwards, Joanna chased both the boys out to play and settled in to an afternoon of baking; on a raw, blustery day, there was nothing she liked better than to fill the kitchen with the yeasty smell of bread dough and the rich fragrance of molasses cookies. She was kneading the bread for the second time, humming a rather tuneless accompaniment to the Saturday afternoon opera on the radio, when there came a sharp tap at the back door. Not wanting to stop what she was doing, she yelled, 'Come in!'

The chorus of *Aida* was swelling in triumphant fortissimo as the back door creaked open and shut and footsteps crossed the porch. Joanna looked up with a welcoming smile, wondering who it was. The door to the kitchen swung open, the man stepped inside, and the smile congealed on her face.

He was as shocked as she—that much was plain. In fact, for what could have been as long as a minute, they stared at each other in total silence, a silence that Stephen Moore finally broke by stating the obvious. 'I didn't realise I'd find *you* here.'

She had had time to recover her wits. 'I'm sure you didn't, or you wouldn't have come, would you? After all, you made it painfully clear that you didn't want to see me again.'

'That's right.'

Perhaps she had hoped he would deny it, or even show a trace of pleasure at meeting her again. Punching the dough down viciously, she said, 'As you're here, I'll give you a cheque to cover the damages to your car.'

'You will not—we already settled that.'

'*You* settled it, you mean!'

'You'll ruin your bread if you keep pounding it so hard.'

Joanna looked down to see a very much flattened piece of dough, and in spite of herself a smile pulled at the corners of her mouth. 'Oh dear, I will, won't I? There's something in you that seems to bring out the worst in me.' Her curiosity getting the best of her, she went on, 'What *are* you doing here?'

'It would seem we're next-door neighbours.'

Her hands grew still on the board. 'You mean you bought the Wintons' house?'

'Yes. I moved in yesterday. I came over to see if I could use your telephone, as mine won't be installed until Monday.'

'Of course you may,' she answered automatically. 'It's through that door in the hall.' Aida's effortless soprano soared into the room. 'You'd either better turn down the radio or shut the door.' He nodded curtly, shutting the door behind him.

Joanna divided the dough into neatly shaped loaves, greased the tops and covered them with a cloth. Then she quickly took a pan of cookies out of the oven, putting in another pan. She was washing her hands at the sink when Stephen Moore came back into the kitchen. He put a two-dollar bill on the table. 'It was a long-distance call, but the operator gave me the charges and that should cover it.'

She glared at him. 'So it's all right for you to give me money, but not the reverse.'

'You're easily the most stubborn creature I've ever met!'

'I was thinking exactly the same of you. However, as I now know where you live, there's nothing to stop me putting a cheque in the mail, is there?' She smiled sweetly. 'And as we're to be neighbours, why don't you sit down and I'll make you a cup of tea? We have ten more minutes of peace and quiet before the boys come back.' Taking his assent for granted, she began to fill the kettle. 'We've all been wondering who'd bought the Wintons' house. It's a beautiful spot, isn't it? Such marvellous trees, and of course the view is the best in the village. Everyone will be anxious to meet you now that you've moved in.'

There was something in the quality of the silence that stopped her artless chatter in midstream. He had not sat down, she saw with a sinking heart.

'I think I'd better make something clear right from

the start,' he said flatly. 'I don't want a stream of people knocking on my door, and I don't particularly want to meet all the neighbours. I came here for privacy. I thought I'd already told you that.'

Her jaw had dropped, and hurriedly she clamped it shut. 'But in the country one often needs one's neighbours. It's different from the city. But that doesn't mean people will be camped on your doorstep the whole time.'

'I came here to finish up a very important job, for which I need to be left alone. And I mean alone. Maybe you wouldn't mind passing the word around.'

Joanna's piquant face froze in disdain, and deliberately she turned the heat off under the kettle. 'You can do your own dirty work, Mr Moore!'

The back door crashed open, twin thuds indicating the discarding of a pair of boots, and Mark burst into the room, his red hair standing up in untidy spikes all over his head. 'The Mercedes you crashed into is in the driveway——' He saw the tall, elegantly dressed stranger standing by the table, and went on almost without a pause, and certainly without waiting for any answers, 'Is it yours? I saw the scratches on it, so I knew it was the same one. Are you mad at her? Hey, are those molasses cookies? Can I have a couple?'

'You may have one,' Joanna said firmly. 'Wash your hands first. The same goes for you, Brian. And you, too, John.'

Her brother grinned at her amiably. 'Nag, nag, nag, the minute I get in the door.' He held out his hand to the other man. 'John Hailey.'

'Stephen Moore. I've moved into the Wintons' house next door. I came here to use your telephone.'

As Joanna supervised Mark's ablutions, a messy business at the best of times, she heard the two men start chatting about, naturally enough, cars, the stranger showing an easy friendliness very different from his manner with her. Then she heard John say,

'Why don't you stay and have supper with us? I'm sure
Jo could rustle up an extra helping, couldn't you, Jo?'

She nodded without much enthusiasm, half prepared
for Stephen Moore's next words. 'That's very kind of
you, but I've already made other arrangements. I have
to get on my way.' He gave Joanna a cool nod and
smiled at John. 'Nice meeting you. Goodbye.'

When John came back in the kitchen, Joanna was
banging the dirty dishes in the sink. He said mildly,
'You didn't seem very keen to have him stay—or did
you only have four pork chops?'

'No, it's stew. But he'd just finished telling me he
didn't want to make friends with any of the
neighbours.'

'He seemed pleasant enough to me.'

'He *was* pleasant enough to you.' She added
flippantly, 'Maybe he's a woman-hater. Would you
rather have beans or broccoli, John?'

Goodnaturedly John accepted the change of subject
and the evening proceeded normally, all four playing
cards until the boys' bedtime, after which Joanna did
some ironing while John brought the farm accounts up
to date. She went upstairs fairly early, for she was tired,
but after she was in bed it was a long while before she
got to sleep; it was difficult to stop thinking about the
stranger, so sophisticated and sure of himself, so
formidably reserved. One thing was sure, she wouldn't
go seeking him out again—she knew when she wasn't
wanted. Maybe, she thought fuzzily, as she eventually
drifted off to sleep, he'd be posting No Trespassing
signs at the entrance to his driveway. . . .

CHAPTER TWO

BECAUSE she was accustomed to the early shift at the hospital where she worked as a laboratory technician, Joanna was awake at six-thirty the next morning. Sunlight was streaming through the chink in her curtains and the wind had died down. She climbed out of bed and opened the curtains. It was a new morning, bright and clean and shining. There were buds on the lilac bushes and in the red maple tree by the barn a song sparrow was practising its trill, its voice thin and reedy, but nevertheless a harbinger of spring.

Joanna didn't even stop to think. She splashed cold water on her face, ran a comb through her hair, and pulled on her jodhpurs and leather boots along with a tight-fitting green turtleneck. Five minutes later she was out in the barn, saddling up Star of the Morning, her bay mare; the horse had had little enough exercise lately, a ride would do her good. With Misty, John's collie, padding along behind, they left the barn.

A wild ride it was, for the spring air seemed to be as intoxicating to Star as it had been to Joanna. They trotted up the path behind the barn, Star nibbling at the bit, and when they reached the hayfield Star broke into a canter that soon became a gallop. The ground rushed by. Exhilarated, out of breath, Joanna bent low over the saddle, feeling the wind whip her cheeks and toss Star's mane back into her face. Through the orchard, down the hill, hooves drumming and leather creaking. Only when they reached the trail that led through the woods to the shore did Joanna rein Star in to a trot and then a walk, giving Misty the chance to catch up with them. They ambled through the trees, last autumn's dead leaves rustling underfoot. There were pussy willows by the creek and tasselled catkins in the alders, and when the three of them emerged on to the shore, a pair of ducks burst into the air. Spring ... Joanna revelled in every tiny sign that announced its coming, for the winters on the Island were long and summer seemed far away.

So headlong had been her ride that she had paid no attention to the fact that along the way they had crossed the boundary between John's property and what was once the Wintons' but now belonged to Stephen Moore. The Wintons had been a cheerful, gregarious couple from Arizona, who had spent every summer on the Island, filling the house with their many children, grandchildren, nieces and nephews, and the Haileys had been encouraged to treat the two properties as one, to use the tennis courts and the beach as if they were their own. So over the years the boundary had almost ceased to exist, and when the Wintons had decided last autumn that the long journey and the big house were finally too much for them, for Jo it had been like losing part of the family.

Now, as she hitched Star to a tree and picked her way over the rocks to the beach, she had no presentiment that she was trespassing; the beach was hers as much as it had ever been, particularly this early on a beautiful morning. Farther out in the bay the pack ice lingered, a dazzling white in the sun, waiting for the offshore winds and the currents to carry it away; but inshore the water was open, gleaming blue and grey like polished metal, rising and falling gently with the swell. Misty gave an expectant bark, her plumed tail waving, her wide jaws grinning.

Joanna grinned back, for this was a time-honoured game. As she stooped and picked up a piece of driftwood from the sand, Misty capered back and forth, barking frenziedly. Using all her strength, Joanna threw the piece of wood up the beach, and like a bullet from a gun Misty was after it. The dog picked it up, carried it back daintily between her jaws, dropped it at Joanna's booted feet, and barked a staccato command. Hurry up! Do it again!

Obligingly Joanna repeated the process, once, twice, half a dozen times, knowing from long experience that Misty would only grow noisier and more insistent with each performance, rather than less so. The game was at its height, Joanna having lobbed the stick almost as far as the rocks at the end of the beach and having yelled at the top of her voice, 'Go get it, Misty! Fetch!', when Star whickered a warning and through the trees came the crash of footsteps. Half expecting it to be one of the boys, Joanna called, 'Come and have a throw—my arm's getting tired!'

The morning light delineated the slender curves of her figure in the green sweater, narrow-fitting leather boots and dark brown jodhpurs, while the sun seemed to catch fire in her hair and in the brilliant depths of her eyes. She was laughing, totally happy, as much a part of her environment as the birds and the trees.

'What the *hell* do you think you're doing?'

It was Stephen Moore. He had burst through the trees to stand only a foot or two away from her, his anger like a dash of ice-cold water in her face. Instinctively Joanna stepped back, the light dying from her eyes. Her heel hit a rock and she might have overbalanced had he not grabbed her by the arm, pulling her closer. He grated, 'I asked you a question!'

'I'm playing with the dog,' she blurted foolishly. 'What's the matter?'

'I could hear the racket you were making up at the house——' Misty had raced back to them and with three loud barks was insisting that the game be re-played. 'Keep that damned dog quiet!'

Joanna stood still. Physically she was very close to Stephen Moore, close enough to see the fan of tiny lines at the corners of his eyes and the marks of a sleepless night etched on his face. Yet she had never felt farther away from anyone in her life. Very quietly, not moving her eyes from his, she said, 'Misty, sit down,' and there must have been something in her voice, for the dog obediently sank down on the sand and began to demolish the stick between her strong, white teeth. Equally quietly Joanna added, 'She won't bark any more now.'

Her face was grave, although her high cheekbones were still dusted with pink from her ride. She knew the next move was up to him and she waited for it, a kind of dignity sitting well on her slim figure.

In the morning stillness with only the soft lap of the waves behind her she heard his harsh, indrawn breath. 'First of all, you're trespassing—this is my land.'

'We're not harming anything. Besides, in a very real sense, I don't think anyone can own the shore and the sea.'

'To get here you had to go through my woods.'

'That's true. The Wintons always allowed us free use of this property.'

'I am not the Wintons.'

'No, that's obvious.'

He swallowed hard. 'Look, I've already told you I came here for peace and quiet, to get away from the noise of the city. So what happens? I'm out on the back verandah trying to work and all I can hear is the dog barking!'

'I'm sorry she disturbed you,' Joanna apologised.

'But you're not sorry you trespassed—is that the message?'

'Yes, I guess it is.' Her face was troubled. 'You keep saying you're trying to get away from it all. Away from what?'

'That's hardly your business.'

'The rest of the world won't stop for you, Mr Moore. People are going to keep on living all around you, and people mean noise and confusion and responsibilities and emotion—you can't escape from all that.'

His fingers tightened around her arm. 'I didn't come down here to listen to a sermon. I came down for two things—to stop that damned dog from barking, and to tell you once and for all that this *is* my property and you and all your family are to stay off it. Do you understand?'

He might just as well not have spoken. 'It's people you're running away from, isn't it?' she whispered. 'You can't *do* that!'

'Oh, for God's sake! Do you go around psychoanalysing everyone you meet?' Naked fury honed his voice, and momentarily the green eyes, dark as her sweater, faltered. 'Get on your horse, take your dog, and go home, Joanna Hailey. And don't come back. I don't want anything more to do with you!'

Joanna had never lacked courage. With her free hand she reached over and detached his fingers from her arm, the brief contact disturbing her more than she would have admitted. 'I'll go,' she said steadily, 'and I won't come back. But you're wrong, you know. You can't turn your back on life.'

For a moment she thought he was going to strike her, and from the dog there came a low, warning growl. 'Come on, Misty,' she said, and walked up the bank to where Star was tethered. It was not until she began to undo the reins that she realised her hands were trembling; as she swung up into the saddle and urged the mare forward with her heels, a blur of tears obscured her vision. Damn the man ... damn him, damn him! He could keep his precious property—she'd never set foot on it again. Star began to trot, and to the rhythm of her hooves the ugly little refrain repeated itself over and over again ... I don't want anything more to do with you, anything more to do with you. ...

A reckless gallop homeward through the orchard and

the field helped a bit. But as Joanna hung up the tack and began to rub Star down, her emotions were still in a turmoil. Anger that she, John, and the boys should be so summarily barred from the woods and beach that they had come to regard almost as their own—yes, she certainly felt that. Personal rejection . . . she felt that, too. In the honesty of her own thoughts Joanna could admit that something about Stephen Moore had attracted her from the start, for he was so radically different from anyone she had ever met before. But he was not attracted by her. Rubbing a bunch of straw over Star's wet flank, she grinned mirthlessly to herself. Oh no, he was not attracted by her. He was repelled by her. He thought she was a self-righteous, sermonising little prig. And maybe she had been. Now that she was back home, her earlier certainty that she was saying the right thing, indeed the only thing to him, had evaporated. How on earth had she ever had the nerve to tell a man like Stephen Moore that he was running away from life? She quivered with embarrassment at the remembrance of it. She must have been mad. . . .

It was a long time since Star had had such a thorough grooming, and the mare, at least, enjoyed it. By the time Joanna was finished, she herself was feeling better, or at any rate more philosophical. What was said was said, and could not be retracted. Her motives had been honest enough, and there was nothing more to be done about it. Except, of course, tell John about the new restriction on their movements.

Her brother took the news surprisingly calmly. 'Well, he's quite within his rights, Jo—the property is his, after all. Over the years we've been exceptionally lucky, but we couldn't expect that to go on for ever. Now, are we going to endeavour to organise these two ruffians and get ourselves off to church?'

For Mark in particular the weekly donning of a suit, shirt, and tie was a major ordeal, and part of the ritual was a vigorous, if useless, protest. Joanna threw herself into the fray and the day proceeded like any other Sunday. Because there was school the next day the boys went to bed early, and regretfully Joanna said to her brother, 'I'd better get going, I suppose. Up at six tomorrow.'

He squeezed her shoulder in one of his rare gestures of affection. 'Thanks, Jo. It sounds trite to say I don't know how I'd manage without you, but I honestly don't. You're a real help—I know the boys miss their mother a lot less because you're here doing things like making cookies and scrubbing behind their ears.'

'It's the least I can do, John. Both you and Sally have made this place like home for me, and I'm sure not every sister-in-law would do that. Did you write to her today?'

'Yeah . . . I write nearly every day. But it's not much of a substitute for seeing her. If only we knew whether the operation had been a success—but it'll be another two weeks before we know that.' He ran his fingers through his hair, which was never tidy at the best of times. 'I hate to think of her up there alone, day after day, helpless in a hospital bed. And what if it doesn't work, Jo? She'll be in a wheelchair for the rest of her life.'

'If it doesn't work, you'll cope with it, both of you,' Joanna said firmly. 'But the neuro-surgeon was quite optimistic, John, you know he was. We'll just have to wait and see.'

Her heart ached for him, for she knew as well as anyone the strong bond between her brother and his wife Sally. Sally, who was in her early thirties, had the most beautiful dark brown eyes that Joanna had ever seen, eyes that were rich in warmth, sensitivity and humour. She adored her tall, easygoing husband and her two young sons, for never far from her mind was the grinding poverty in which she had grown up in an isolated logging camp in New Brunswick, the chain of events that had led to her chance meeting with John at an agricultural exhibition, and their instant recognition of each other as the one person needed for completion. They were indeed the two halves of a whole, and even after thirteen years of marriage the flame burned as brightly as it had that first day under the glaring sun in the show ring. They had not always been easy years, for John was building up the market gardens and orchards that were his livelihood, while Sally was increasingly plagued by spinal problems that eventually necessitated her spending weeks flat on her back. She had gone from specialist to specialist, until a month ago she had seen a world-renowned surgeon in Montreal who had felt that an operation carried a fair chance of success. During Sally's absence Joanna had been commuting back and forth between the farm and her apartment in town, helping as much as she could just as she had when Sally had been immobilised at home.

John tweaked her ear. 'Drive carefully, won't you, Sis? What's your schedule for the rest of the week?'

'I can come here tomorrow after work. Tuesday Drew and I have tickets for a play at Confederation Centre.'

'Behave yourself,' he grinned.

She wrinkled her nose at him. 'Don't I always?' In a sudden rush of honesty she added, 'The trouble is, I'm not really tempted to do otherwise with Drew.'

'He's a good-looking guy,' John said judiciously. 'A good doctor, too.'

'I know. Maybe it's me . . . perhaps I'm just too fussy. The trouble is I've never met anyone who makes me feel even a fraction of what you and Sally seem to feel for each other. And having seen the two of you together, I won't settle for less.'

'Too bad our new neighbour is so unfriendly.'

'Oh, him. . . .' Joanna grimaced. 'He doesn't even want to see me again, he made that horribly clear this morning.'

'Well, you know, Sis, you're only twenty-three. Not quite on the shelf yet.'

'When you were twenty-three, you and Sally were married.'

'Perhaps you and Drew need a little more time. After all, you've only been dating him for four or five months.'

'Perhaps ... I really must go, John.' She kissed him on the cheek. 'Take care, and I'll see you tomorrow around four. Don't forget to take something out of the freezer for supper.'

'I won't. 'Bye, Jo.'

It was a forty-minute drive to Joanna's apartment in town, one of a dozen flats in a utilitarian brick building that had as its main advantage its location on a pleasant, tree-lined side street only a five-minute walk from the hospital. She slept like a log, for her weekends at the farm were anything but restful, and the alarm jolted her out of a deep sleep. She showered, dressed in her uniform, had breakfast, and walked to work. There had been a silver thaw; frost lay heavily on the grass and the naked tree limbs, the crystals sparkling in the dawn sunlight, and Joanna drew deep breaths of the chill air, glad to be alive.

She went in the side door of the hospital, with its unmistakable atmosphere of disinfectant and overheated corridors, and as soon as she passed through the swing doors to the laboratory, the routine claimed her. Because they were understaffed she was kept busy the whole day, although she did manage to snatch a quick lunch in the cafeteria with Drew, where they confirmed their plans for the following evening.

On Tuesday it made a pleasant change to go straight to her apartment from work. She drew a hot bath and soaked the tiredness from her body, washed her hair and did her nails. Her dress was full-skirted and wide-sleeved, bright taffeta roses on a dark background that rustled as she walked; gold hoop earrings, supple leather boots, and—her one extravagance of last winter—a cream-coloured mohair coat completed her outfit. Leaving her coat on the chair, she carefully applied a dusting of gold and green eyeshadow and a very pale lipstick, then pirouetted in front of the mirror, enjoying the swish of the taffeta. What would Stephen Moore think if he could see her now? That she was still an unsophisticated country girl, someone to be shoved aside? Probably. . . .

The doorbell rang and she ran to open it. 'Hi, Drew, come in. I'm actually ready on time!'

Dr Drew Cartwright was a stickler for punctuality, for he liked his life to be orderly and well run. Tonight, as always, his grooming was impeccable, the crease in his trousers knife-sharp, his shoes polished to a mirror-like shine. In Joanna's somewhat muddled thinking, it was Drew's excessive neatness that bothered her as much as anything. She had few illusions about herself: she was impulsive and untidy, and always enjoyed the unexpected. Drew might laugh indulgently at her wayward habits, but she had a feeling that were they ever to marry, that laughter might wear a bit thin. On the credit side, for she would not have gone out with him had she not genuinely liked him, he was a conscientious and concerned doctor who managed to maintain an active interest in the arts. Besides which, she thought mischievously, his profile could easily have adorned an ancient gold medallion, so classically handsome was he.

'You look beautiful, honey.' He kissed her firmly on the lips, then stepped back. 'Mmm, you smell nice, too.'

'It's the perfume you gave me for my birthday. Oh look, I've got lipstick on you—stand still.' As she scrubbed at his mouth with a tissue, she wondered, not for the first time, if the fault for her lack of response lay with her. She liked his kisses, for they were pleasant enough. But that was all. No stars fell from the heavens, she was seized by no uncontrollable urges. It was simply nice to be kissed by him . . . and what a dreadful word 'nice' could be under such circumstances! she thought ruefully.

Drew helped her into her coat, she checked that she had her keys in her purse, and they were off. He had booked a table at their favourite restaurant, another evidence of his thoughtfulness, and Joanna thoroughly enjoyed her dinner. 'So nice not to have cooked it, and to know someone else will take away the dirty plates and wash them.'

'Quite selfishly, I'll be glad when Sally is home and back to normal. You're working too hard, Joanna. I know how demanding your job is, and it's not much of a rest afterwards to drive twenty miles and take on the housework for a family.'

No doubt he was right, but there was nothing could be done about it. 'An evening like this every now and then is just what the doctor ordered,' she replied, a twinkle in her eye. 'How's the time? Had we better be going?'

The play was a frothy and very funny bit of nonsense about three couples whose business and love affairs had become inextricably entwined, and Joanna laughed until she cried. It was nearly eleven o'clock by the time they edged their way to the exit and out into the raw April night. Jostled by the crowds, Joanna felt herself shivering after the warmth of the theatre. 'I don't think summer's ever going to come,' she complained.

'Dreadful climate, isn't it?' Drew agreed cheerfully, putting an arm around her shoulders. 'Want a drink before we go home?'

'Why not?' Suddenly feeling very fond of him, and forgetting the crowd all around them, she impetuously stood on tiptoes and kissed his cheek. 'Thanks, Drew, I've really enjoyed this evening.'

Someone jostled them hard, so that Drew said jokingly, 'You do choose your moments for getting romantic, honey. . . . Why's that fellow staring at us—do you know him?'

Looking over the crowd it was no trouble to pick out whom Drew had meant, for the man stood head and shoulders above most of the other theatregoers. Joanna felt her heart give an uncomfortable flip-flop, for it was Stephen Moore. She had seen him angry before, but this time there was more than anger in his face as he stared at her and her companion across the forty or fifty feet of pavement that separated them: there was a corrosive contempt that made her physically flinch backwards into the shelter of Drew's arm. 'It's our new neighbour at the farm,' she whispered. 'Why is he looking at me like that?' Even as she spoke Stephen Moore turned on his heel and began walking away from them, soon to be lost in the traffic.

'A tough-looking customer,' Drew commented. 'How did you get in his bad books?'

'Oh, I drove into his car, and then he caught me trespassing on his property,' she said drearily, all her pleasure in the evening destroyed.

'That could explain it,' was Drew's dry response.

Joanna did not agree, but she was not about to argue. More shaken than she wanted Drew to see, for that one look seemed to have flayed the skin from her body, she said, with attempted lightness, 'How about that drink? Then we'd better head home, I'm on the early shift again tomorrow.'

Try as she might Joanna was unable to forget the ugly little incident; over the next few days those searing grey eyes would suddenly force themselves upon her vision. The only consolation was that Stephen Moore made no more appearances at the farm. The weekend came and went in the usual flurry of activity and then it was Monday again and back to the lab. On Thursday night Joanna was on call, and then had to work all day Friday; it was four-thirty before she pulled into the driveway at the farm, and the first thing she saw was a black Mercedes parked by the barn. John and Stephen Moore were standing beside it, talking with every appearance of amicability.

Joanna was very tired, and somehow this seemed like

the last straw. She parked her car as far from the Mercedes as she could and got out. When John beckoned her over, there was no disguising the reluctance with which she approached the two men. She was still in uniform, a slim-fitting white tunic and trousers with her gold name-plate on her left breast; there were shadows under her eyes, while her red hair seemed to have drained all the colour from her face. John put an arm around her shoulders. 'You look worn out,' he said gently.

'I guess I am . . . where are the boys?'

'Playing at the Arsenaults'.'

Because, short of outright rudeness, Joanna did not seem to have much choice, she said coolly, 'Hello, Mr Moore.' As he acknowledged her greeting with a very slight inclination of his head, his eyes like stones, she felt pure rage lick like a flame within her. She forced it down, forced herself to reply to John's, 'Bad day?'

'Dreadful,' she said succinctly. 'I was on call last night—a motorbike accident, a heart attack, and an emergency appendectomy. Today wasn't much better. And I have to work on Sunday.'

'Then this evening you're going to sit with your feet up and do nothing, do you hear me?'

'Yes, sir,' she answered pertly. A yawn escaped her, and childishly she rubbed at her eyes. 'I expect I'll be in bed by nine o'clock.'

They all three heard the telephone ring in the house, a faint, shrill summons. 'Excuse me a sec,' John said quickly.

'I think we're finished anyway, John,' Stephen Moore intervened equally quickly.

Running towards the house, John called back, 'No, hold on a minute—there's somethng else I wanted to ask you.'

Her anger burst into life again, only this time Joanna did not bother trying to hide it. Her green eyes blazing, she snapped, 'Don't worry, you don't have to stand around being polite to me, that's the last thing I expect from you. But you can tell me one thing—do you hate all women on general principle, or is it only me?'

'This is hardly the time or the place for you to ask a question like that.'

'I fail to see why.'

'When your husband could appear back on the scene at any moment?'

'My—what?' She couldn't have heard correctly.

'Oh, for God's sake,' he said irritably, 'you heard what I said. Why don't you drop that wide-eyed, innocent look—I'm not in the mood for playing games. You're a two-timing litt.e bitch playing around with another man behind your husband's back. I've seen lots of your kind, I don't know why it should bother me so much—perhaps because John is such a thoroughly nice guy.'

'John is not my husband,' Joanna said clearly. 'He's my brother.'

It was his turn to look as though the earth had rocked beneath his feet. 'Your *brother*?'

'Yes.' Somehow she felt as though she had to keep talking, to give him time to recover from what appeared to be a severe shock. 'He's twelve years older than I. There were only the two of us in the family.'

'So is he a widower?'

'Goodness, no. But his wife's in hospital in Montreal. She's been there for nearly a month now, and it will be at least another month before she gets home.' Briefly she described the nature of Sally's illness. 'So that's why I'm here so much, to try and keep things on a more or less even keel.'

Still speaking as though his mind was only half on what he was saying, he asked, 'You're a nurse?'

'No, a lab technician. Generally I work the seven to three shift, so that gives me time to get up here after work and give John a hand with the meals and the housework.' She hesitated. 'I can't understand why

John never mentioned Sally to you—his whole world revolves around her and the boys.'

'I never asked, for one thing.' His lips twisted. 'I don't encourage enquiries about my own personal life, so I suppose the other side of the coin is that I don't ask other people about theirs.'

'I have noticed that about you, now that you mention it,' she said impishly. Reverting back, she added, 'I don't wear a wedding ring.'

'A lot of women don't nowadays.' His brow furrowed. 'It was a combination of a whole lot of things, when I look back, Joanna—you don't mind if I call you that, do you?'

'I prefer it, Mr Moore,' she replied demurely.

'Stephen, please.'

She felt as though a giant step forward had been taken, and the whole world suddenly seemed a brighter, sunnier place, her weariness sliding away from her. 'You were saying?'

'Well, the first time we met you mentioned John with the kind of casualness that goes with a long acquaintance ... it was his car, he was used to you getting into scrapes, and so on. And then when I came to the house to use the telephone, it was all so overpoweringly domesticated. You were making bread—how did it turn out, by the way?'

That glint of humour was irresistible. 'It was tough.'

'I'm not surprised, the beating you were giving it. And then the boys and John came in, and you were so obviously a family ... you can hardly blame me for drawing the conclusions I did.'

'No ... I can see how it could have happened. So when you saw me with Drew outside the theatre the other night you thought I was stepping out on John.' A flush touched her cheeks as she remembered how she had reached up and kissed Drew so publicly.

'Exactly.' He said stiffly, 'I owe you an apology, Joanna. I've been very rude to you.'

She held out her hand, her green eyes direct. 'Your apology is accepted, Stephen.' As he briefly clasped her hand in his, she had the sense that something momentous had happened. It was almost a relief to hear the bang of the screen door and to see John standing on the back porch. Hurriedly she freed her hand and together they walked down the slope towards the house.

Very matter-of-factly Stephen said, 'We've just been sorting out a misunderstanding.' He smiled down at Joanna, a smile that did funny things to her heart. 'I was under the totally erroneous impression that Joanna was your wife.'

'My wife?' A wide grin split John's face. 'Good lord, man, have a heart—she gives me enough trouble as my sister!' He gave Joanna a rough hug, and she laughed up at him, the affection between them as bright and sure as the rising of the sun. John looked back at the other man. 'You mean I never mentioned Sally to you?'

'I'm positive you didn't.'

'Strange ... that was her on the phone. The physiotherapy's going very well, so everyone's being a bit more optimistic.' His face clouded. 'She still has a lot of pain, though. I'll be so damned glad when this is over and she's home again.'

Joanna linked her arm with his. 'I'll make you a cup of tea before I start supper.' Anything to erase that look of strain, borne too long, from his face. 'Why don't you join us, Stephen?' she offered, his name slipping as easily from her tongue as if she had been saying it for weeks.

'No, I won't, thanks. The last load of books arrived yesterday, so I've been trying to get my study in order. Are all our arrangements made, John?'

'All but the date.'

'I don't know that for sure myself—probably by the middle of next week.'

Piqued that he could be so at ease with John but

would not stay and have a cup of tea with her, and mystified by the conversation, Joanna asked, 'Arrangements for what?'

'John's being kind enough to board my horse in your barn for a month or so, until I can get something built at my place—the Wintons seem to have had everything from a sauna to a croquet lawn, but no stables.'

Joanna chuckled. 'Emily Winton hated horses. According to her one end was apt to bite and the other end to kick, while the middle was far too high off the ground.'

'That's one way of looking at a horse, I suppose. John, I'll give you a call as soon as I hear anything further.' A nod in Joanna's general direction, and he was striding away from them towards his car.

Once inside, Joanna put the kettle on. 'I wish he'd stayed,' she said to her brother in a small voice. 'He seems to spend an awful lot of time alone.'

'That must be his choice, Sis.'

'Mmm. . . .' She was conscious of tiredness again, of muscles that ached and eyes that burned.

'He'll probably come round in time. After all, if he's going to keep his horse here, he'll be back and forth a lot more often.'

She hadn't thought of that . . . with a new briskness she dropped the tea-bags in the pot and got out the mugs. 'What else did Sally have to say?' As John began relating the conversation in more detail, Joanna thankfully sank into a chair, forcing herself to pay attention to him rather than allowing herself to remember her conversation with Stephen. She did not have time to mull over that until she went to her room later in the evening, by which time she was so tired that her only conclusion was that from now on things would somehow be different between her and Stephen Moore. He had thought her a married woman; he now knew she was not. That had to make a difference . . . didn't it? Her head burrowed itself into the pillow and within seconds she was asleep.

CHAPTER THREE

JOANNA had never noticed before how slowly the days could pass when subconsciously one was waiting for a phone call or a visit, neither of which materialised. As if to mock her hopes, unexpressed to anyone save herself, spring was gathering force. The chorus of birdsong was more varied and more convincing every morning; the maples were in flower, tiny new tassels misting the trees with colour; the fields were drying and patches of bright green grass sprang up in sheltered hollows in the ground. And finally the swallows had returned, tumbling and swooping in the tentative May sunshine.

Normally all this would have been calculated to make Joanna sing as she went about her chores. But this year spring's arrival only seemed to accentuate a restlessness whose roots she could not understand, a dissatisfaction with her daily routine, and in particular with her dates with Drew, that left her edgy and out of sorts. The arrival of Stephen's horse was delayed; Sally developed, of all things, a severe intestinal 'flu that set her back several days, as one result of which even John's normal good temper was frayed. Maybe the boys were only reacting to the unspoken tensions in the house when Mark deliberately spilled fruit juice on Brian's homework, and easygoing Brian threw the sodden papers in his brother's face. Mark's wailed, 'I want my Mummy!' as he was carted upstairs by his father, cut Joanna to the quick. Nothing seemed to have gone right since Stephen Moore had moved in next door, she thought in an illogical flash of irritation. It was as if his unseen presence was casting a shadow over them all. . . .

She sat sunk in gloom for a moment longer, then her sense of humour got the better of her; she was acting

41

like a Gothic heroine, blaming everything on the hero—
or was he the villain? The mental image of Stephen
Moore as a black-browed villain further restored her
equanimity. She'd go to the store and buy some
chocolate, and make the boys a cake with lots of icing.
There was nothing like a chocolate cake for cheering
one up. Grabbing her keys from the hutch, she called
her intention to John and ran outside. The wind tugged
at her denim skirt, moulding her blouse to her figure,
and the cloud of depression that seemed to have been
hanging over her for days suddenly lifted.

A few moments later she wondered if her change of
mood had not been a premonition. Running down the
worn wooden steps of the general store with her parcel
in her arms, she saw a black Mercedes turn into the
parking lot and pull up beside her own car. Stephen
Moore got out, saw her, and waited to speak to her.
She did not stop to analyse the lift of her heart. 'Hello!'
she called.

'Hello, Joanna. How are you?'

'Fine,' she beamed, forgetting that half an hour ago
she had been far from fine. On impulse she added,
'Stephen, why don't you come and have supper with us?
The Arsenaults brought us some scallops and I'm going
to make a chocolate cake. Do come!'

He looked down into her vibrant, heart-shaped face.
Afterwards she was to wonder if she had imagined the
pleasure that all too briefly crossed his face. Then he
shook his head slowly. 'No, Joanna.'

'Why not?'

He hesitated. then abruptly seemed to come to a
decision. 'I could give you some kind of a polite excuse,
I suppose, but I'm not going to do that. I think you
deserve the truth.'

She waited, wondering what on earth he was going to
say, her hands unconsciously tightening on the bag of
groceries.

'I don't know if I can explain it to you,' he began.

'I'm not even sure I fully understand it myself. I just don't want to get involved.'

'Involved?' she repeated, searching his sombre features for clues. 'I—I don't understand. Involved with whom?'

'With you, mostly.'

'With me?' All she seemed to be capable of was repeating his words back to him, she thought numbly.

'To a lesser extent with your family. But it's mainly you. You're a lovely young woman, Joanna, and I find you very attractive, but you deserve better than I.'

'Surely I should have some say in that.'

'No. I'd be no good for you.'

She shifted the parcel in her arms, knowing that it was desperately important that she understand him. Deciding to try shock tactics, she said bluntly, 'Are you married? Is that what you mean?'

'No, I'm divorced . . . I may even be widowed for all I know.'

It was his first slip, for there had been raw emotion in his voice. 'You don't know where she is?' Joanna said carefully.

The words forced themselves from his throat. 'I don't know if she's alive or dead.'

'You still love her.'

'I don't even know that any more.' He rubbed at his forehead with fingers that were not quite steady. 'I don't want to talk about her. But she's the reason why I won't come with you this evening, Joanna, or even be friends on a casual basis. I've nothing to give you.'

Her throat was tight with tension, the strain of the conversation beginning to tell on her. Picking her words with care, because it seemed important to be absolutely honest with him, she said, 'Shouldn't you try and get over her?'

'It's not that simple.'

'Oh.' She shrugged helplessly. 'Then I'm sorry. I would have liked to get to know you better, Stephen. You're different from anyone I've ever met before.'

'It's nice of you to say that.' Fleetingly his hand rested on her shoulder, and every nerve ending in her body quivered into life. He said gently, 'Take care of yourself, you look tired.'

'I will.' She had to end this, because she knew, shamefully, that she was going to cry. 'I must go. Goodbye.'

'Goodbye.'

He moved away from her, his lean hips and long legs carrying him with easy grace up the slope to the store, and she took a moment to realise what an incongruous setting this had been for such a dialogue: a dusty parking lot where a motley collection of candy wrappers danced and spun in the wind, and garish billboards advertised cigarettes, soft drinks, and bread. The paint was peeling off the store front, she noticed abstractedly, trying hard to blink back the tears. She'd better get out of here before he came back.

By the time Joanna drew up at the farmhouse, the urge to cry had passed; she was left instead with a dull ache located somewhere in her midriff—was that where her heart was kept? she wondered, with a grim attempt at humour. As soon as she stepped inside the door, the domestic routine claimed her, but she had long ago discovered that while housework might busy the hands, it left the mind free to wander. As she creamed the butter and sugar and beat the eggs, she thought back over everything Stephen had said. He had done his best to be honest with her, and that in itself was a kind of compliment; and he found her attractive. But the past, in the form of his ex-wife, exercised a more powerful hold on him than she, Joanna, did; perhaps he had sensed that she was attracted to him, and was dealing with her in the kindest way possible.

As she beat in the flour, her predominant emotion was one of having been cheated. It was as if a door had opened just a chink, enough to let her catch a quick glimpse of an unimaginably beautiful garden; then, just as she was about to open the door further so that she could step through, the door had been slammed in her face. What had occurred between her and Stephen Moore since the first day they had met? Anger and discord. A rare smile, a brief touch, the memory of which would remain with her for the rest of her life. And that was all. He had never offered her anything else. He had made no advances, held out no promises. Almost from the beginning he had shunned her. So the hurt she was feeling stemmed from herself; inexplicably, and against all the dictates of common sense, the dark-haired stranger had found a way into her heart that Drew, for instance, had never found. In love? She couldn't be in love! She scarcely knew Stephen Moore, had never gone out with him or been kissed by him . . . yet just to think of him kissing her sent a strange shiver of excitement through her body. Her hands grew still. You couldn't fall in love with a man you didn't know—could you?

A rather subdued Mark asked if he could scrape out the bowl and John began breading the scallops. In a voice she tried to make offhand, Joanna said, 'John, when you met Sally, how soon did you know she was the one you wanted to marry?'

She was busying herself with the deep-fryer, so she missed the quick glance of speculation John sent her way. 'Right away,' he said cheerfully. 'I was showing a heifer in the ring and I looked up and there was this girl with dark curls and big brown eyes leaning on the fence watching me. I let go of the rope, the heifer took off, and I was eliminated from the class. Nobody else could figure out why I'd done something so stupid, because I was the favourite for first place—but she and I knew.'

'So you both knew,' she said wistfully.

'Yes . . . we were lucky. I'm sure it doesn't always happen that way.'

'No, I don't suppose it does. Mark, you'll take the pattern off the bowl if you scrape any harder!'

With innate tact John followed her lead and they chatted about commonplaces as the meal cooked. After the boys were in bed, homework done and teeth brushed, Joanna rather ostentatiously picked up a book she was reading; while she often confided in John, Stephen's quietly spoken ultimatum seemed too new, too intimate, to share even with someone as close to her as her brother.

Two days later when she arrived at the farm after work and dashed in the house to get out of the rain, Joanna knew something was wrong the minute she came into the kitchen. John could not have heard her car, for he was sitting at the table with his head buried in his hands. He looked up as she entered and she was shocked by his haggard appearance. 'What's wrong?' she blurted.

'I've got a hell of a headache. I sent the boys over to the Arsenaults to play.'

Joanna sat down across from him; this had happened two or three times before. 'You've been worrying about Sally,' she chided him gently.

'She's still in such a lot of pain . . . if I could only bear it for her, I would.'

'Of course you would,' Joanna said calmly. 'John, it's time you went up to see her.'

'Do you think I don't know that?' he said in an agony of frustration. 'But I can't, Jo. There just isn't the money. The orchards didn't do that well last year, I had to get a new motor for the sprayer and a new water pump, and there's been all the extra expense of the private room at the hospital. I'd need my plane fare and I'd have to stay in a hotel. It just can't be done.'

They had had this argument before, but perhaps this time John was desperate enough that he'd listen to reason. 'All I'd have to do is defer one month's payment on my car at the bank and that would be enough for you to fly to Montreal. Please let me do it,

John ... please! It's as important for Sally as it is for you.'

'Jo, we've been through all this before. You do far too much for me already, I can't take your money on top of everything else. For God's sake, leave me a bit of pride!'

He had raised his voice so that neither of them heard the back door open and close. 'Pride!' Joanna flared. 'What's pride got to do with it? You and Sally need to *see* each other—money is just the means to an end. Don't you see that, John? Sally's more important than money.'

'Of course she is,' he said angrily. 'But I won't take your money, Jo—and that's that.'

'You're so damned stubborn! I'm tempted to get the money anyway and go ahead and make your booking——'

'So help me, Jo, if you do that, I'll——'

The sharp rap on the half-open kitchen door made both their heads swing round. In the sudden silence Stephen Moore stepped into the room, his shrewd grey eyes missing not one detail of John's ruffled hair and obstinately set chin, or of Joanna's flushed face, passionate with the intensity of her feelings. He was wearing a raincoat, beaded with moisture, and his hair was curling damply on his forehead. Without bothering to sound particularly apologetic he said, 'I'm sorry, I seem to be interrupting something. I might as well admit that I heard a considerable amount of your—er—discussion. I did knock at the back door, but no one seemed to hear ... I have my pilot's licence and a friend just flew my plane down to the Charlottetown airport the other day, where it's sitting gathering dust. It would be doing me a favour if you'd let me take you up to Montreal and back, John—I need to log some more hours.'

'It would take up too much of your time,' John said uncertainly.

'I was planning on doing a long run this weekend, anyway.' For the first time Stephen hesitated. 'But would you be free to look after the boys, Joanna?'

'I have Saturday and Sunday off, and one of the other girls owes me a day, so I could ask her if she'd work the early shift on Monday for me,' she replied promptly.

Stephen's face cleared. 'That's okay, then. What do you say, John?'

Joanna held her breath. Would he accept Stephen's offer, or would his pride get in the way again? 'You're sure you were planning a flight anyway?' John asked. Stephen nodded. John looked down at his work-stained hands resting on the table. 'I could surprise her,' he said quietly. 'Just walk into her room and surprise her.'

Joanna held her tongue; it was Stephen who said with just the right degree of casualness, 'You'll come, then?'

As John's hazel eyes locked with Stephen's cool grey ones, some wholly masculine message was exchanged between them. 'Thanks,' said John. 'I accept with pleasure. When would we go?'

'How about first thing Saturday morning?'

'Great!' A wide grin split John's face and he suddenly looked ten years younger. 'Hey, this calls for a drink. What have we got, Sis?'

'There's some beer in the refrigerator and I think there's sherry in the cupboard.'

As John got up to get glasses, he tweaked Joanna's hair. 'Sorry I yelled at you, Jo.'

'I think I did my fair share of the yelling, too.' They smiled at each other and the subject was closed.

Stephen did not stay long; as he was leaving Joanna managed to get a few words alone with him, for John had gone to pick up the boys. The rain was drumming on the porch roof and in the gloom her uniform was the only patch of brightness. Wanting to touch him yet obscurely afraid to do so, she contented herself with saying, 'Thank you so much, Stephen. This will make the world of difference to John, and to Sally, too.'

'They mean a lot to each other, don't they?'

'The whole world,' she agreed warmly.

In the small, overcrowded porch he looked very big, his hands thrust in his pockets, his shoulders hunched. She wanted to cry out, 'Don't go back to that big, empty house—stay here with us!' but he himself had forbidden her to do that. But before she could lose courage, she did say, 'Don't you get lonely over there sometimes?'

'I'm used to being alone.'

'That's not really answering my question.'

'Of course I get lonely. But don't we all? Even with your job and your friends and your family, don't you get lonely sometimes, Joanna?'

'Yes.'

Her quietly spoken answer seemed to hang in the air between them. He made a sudden movement towards her, then just as suddenly halted, tension in every line of his body. A trick of the light turned his features into a monochromatic mask: deep-sunk black eyes, dark gash of mouth, thick hair black as night. She waited, her heartbeat echoing in her ears, her whole body aching for his touch.

The silence stretched out, singing with its own tension. When Stephen finally spoke, his voice was rough. 'The friend you were with at the theatre—you looked to be on good terms with him. Why don't you marry him? Then you wouldn't be lonely.'

The truth was crystal clear in her mind. 'Yes, I would be. Because I don't love him. I like him, I enjoy his company, and he's a fine doctor—but I don't love him.'

'Don't think love is the pretty affair of red roses and moonlight that society would have us believe. If you like him and respect him, then maybe you're better off. Marry him, and be happy.'

'I can't, Stephen. I——' There was no delicate way of

putting it, yet it had to be said. 'The chemistry's not right. When I kiss him—oh, it's pleasant, it's nice, but nothing more than that. I haven't the slightest desire to make love with him.' She spread her hands helplessly. 'It's crazy, really. I'm the envy of all the nursing staff because I'm dating Drew Cartwright, the handsomest and most eligible doctor in the county. Maybe there's something wrong with me . . . I don't know.'

'You must have made love before. . . .'

'No. No, I never have.'

'I wish you hadn't told me that, Joanna.' He paused. 'From the first moment I met you, I've wanted to make love to you.'

Her hands dropped to her sides. He was standing five feet away from her and with the sureness of intuition she knew he would not, physically, touch her. But the words he had spoken had been as palpable as a touch. As if he had reached out a hand and stroked her, her whole body came sweetly to life . . . he wanted to make love to her. Had wanted to from the first moment he had seen her. She said irrelevantly, 'I looked dreadful that day—that awful old jacket and my muddy boots!'

'Fishing for compliments?'

Her laugh was delightful. 'No!' But then she sobered, because she knew with a curious sense of foreboding that everything had been said. He wanted to make love to her, but he would not do so, would not make the slightest of advances, all because of a self-imposed vow whose origins she did not understand. And what of herself? What did she want? Was he the man whom subconsciously she had been waiting for, the one who would assuage the restlessness, the strange longings she felt when she saw skeins of wild geese span the sky with their wings?

From outside, over the beat of rain, came the crunch of tyres in the gravel and the slam of car doors. 'Goodnight, Joanna,' said Stephen with a finality she had come to expect.

'Goodnight,' she whispered. Then the porch was full of small boys and wet clothes, and Misty had pushed her way in out of the rain, and John was giving orders, and the moments of intimacy were shattered. For intimacy it had been, she thought, hanging up Mark's raincoat on one of the hooks. It was as if something in Stephen forbade him to treat her with anything less than honesty, no matter how shocking that honesty might be. . . .

'Can Lisette come over here tomorrow after school?' Mark was clamouring, and Joanna forced herself back to the present. Lisette was the youngest of the Arsenaults' six children and lived on the farm to the east of them. She was a chubby, doe-eyed child who adored Mark, trailing behind him wherever he went and all too frequently coerced into whatever mischief he was up to.

'If it's all right with her mother, she may,' Joanna responded with a degree of prudence she had learned over the years in her dealings with Mark. 'Go and wash your hands.'

'What's for supper?'

She didn't have the faintest idea. 'Leftovers,' she said vaguely.

John grinned at her. 'It's okay, I took some pork chops out of the freezer. Why don't you sit down, Jo, and I'll get supper started.'

'Maybe I'll go and get out of my uniform and have a shower.'

'What were you and Stephen talking about? He stayed for quite a while.'

Taken off balance, she felt colour scorch her cheeks. 'Oh, nothing much,' she mumbled, picking up her handbag and beating a hasty retreat before he could ask anything else.

CHAPTER FOUR

EVEN though she knew it would be a meeting of only a few minutes, Joanna found herself looking forward to seeing Stephen on Saturday morning with a degree of anticipation that rather frightened her; she'd wear her denim jumpsuit with a silk scarf tucked in the neckline; it was practical, yet becoming at the same time. She went to bed early Friday night, feeling more tired than she should have been considering it had been a relatively easy day at the lab; the minute she woke up on Saturday, she knew something was wrong. She felt dizzy and sick, cold one minute and hot the next. Cautiously getting out of bed, she looked at herself in the mirror in consternation. Circles under her eyes, skin stretched tight across her cheekbones, dead-white face. She looked terrible, and felt worse. But she couldn't let John down, she simply couldn't . . . if he realised she was ill, he wouldn't go to Montreal, she knew him well enough for that. So he mustn't find out.

Taking a few deep breaths to try and calm her racing pulse, she walked steadily across the hall to the bathroom. A shower brought a little colour to her cheeks, although she had to fight back an attack of violent shivering as she got dressed in the jumpsuit, substituting a scarf in subtle tones of pink and mauve for the vivid orange one she had originally planned on wearing. Eyeshadow, a careful application of blusher, and lipstick did wonders for her complexion, and to the passing eye, she decided, she would look much as normal.

Fortunately John was far too excited to pay much attention to her, or to the fact that she only nibbled at her toast. He looked unaccustomedly smart in beige slacks and a tweed jacket, his pleasantly angular face very tanned above an off-white shirt. 'I'll call you from the hotel tonight, Sis. Mark, don't forget you're responsible for feeding the chickens and gathering the eggs, and Brian, you'll feed the heifers and get milk from the Arsenaults.'

Mark had been watching through the window for Stephen to arrive, although Joanna suspected he was more interested in the Mercedes than in its driver. 'He's here, Dad!'

They all went outside, Joanna trailing behind, for she felt horribly dizzy. In the porch she bent to straighten the boys' boots, letting the blood rush to her head, then cautiously straightening. That felt better. Another few minutes and she'd be safe. . . .

Stephen had given Mark the keys to open the back of the station wagon and John heaved his suitcase inside, tossing his raincoat in with it. Then as he stooped to hug his sons, Stephen walked around the car to where Joanna was standing, purposely in the shadow of the house, her arms hugged across her breast. 'Good morning,' she said brightly. 'It should be a lovely day for flying.'

He glanced up at the pale blue sky, dotted with a few fluffy white clouds. 'Made to order. I'll take good care of him, Joanna.'

Grimly she fought back a wave of shivering. 'I'm sure you will.'

'There's a possibility my horse may arrive over the weekend. If so, I'll give you a ring.'

'Fine.' Just go, she willed him fiercely, and briefly his sun-edged image slid into two, then three, wavered and dipped.

'Are you all right?'

She opened her eyes wide. 'Of course I am. Hadn't you better go? I don't want the boys getting upset by a long goodbye.'

He was frowning, and it took John's, 'Ready,

Stephen?' to make him turn away from her, his parting words, prosaically enough, 'Don't work too hard this weekend—you look as if you could do with a break.'

The two boys stood very close to Joanna as the Mercedes reversed down the driveway. Mark tucked his hand into hers. 'I wish we could have gone, too,' he gulped.

'I'm sure you do, love. But your mum's getting better, you know, and she'll be home by the time school ends.'

'That's ages away!'

'You'll be surprised how quickly it will go.' Knowing both boys needed distraction, because even Brian looked unusually subdued, she said, 'Tell you what, we'll go to the store and buy you each a new Dinkie toy, and maybe even a chocolate bar to go with it. Then you could play up in the sandpit as it's such a nice day.'

This scheme was approved of, and within an hour both boys were happily rearranging the sandpit into a complicated network of roads and bridges that would have been an engineer's nightmare. Sheer relief at having John safely out of the way had made Joanna feel better for a while, and by a mixture of firm determination and a judicious series of rests, she managed to get through the day without the boys realising anything was amiss; by seven o'clock that evening they were settled in front of the television in the living room. By now Joanna had a splitting headache, for she had eaten very little all day in response to recurring attacks of nausea; by surreptitiously taking her temperature she had discovered she had a fever—not that she had really needed a thermometer to tell her that. Going upstairs was an effort, each step as tall as a mountain. She got undressed, putting on a fleecy, peach-coloured negligee lavishly edged with lace, that temporarily raised her morale. But when she removed her make-up, she regarded herself in the mirror with disfavour. She looked like a clown, a white face with crude patches of colour high on the cheekbones.

Normally not much of a television fan, tonight she was content to curl up on the chesterfield with pillows heaped behind her back and an eiderdown covering her, and blessedly no chores to be done. At nine she sent the boys upstairs, gave them long enough to get themselves into bed, and then dragged herself up there to tuck them in. Although they had been very little trouble all day, it was still a great relief to know that until tomorrow she had only herself to look after. She could go to bed now . . . thank goodness.

But then as she crossed the hallway to her room she heard the sound of voices downstairs . . . she'd left the television on. And all the lights . . . oh, damn. Down the stairs again, holding tightly to the banister, for the whole room had a tendency to heave up and down as though she was adrift in a boat. By the time she reached the chesterfield, her face was bathed in perspiration and her heart was pounding in her ears. She'd lie down for a minute before she started the trek back up the stairs again, she thought fuzzily. Sinking down on the pillows, she pulled the quilt up to her chin, and closed her eyes. . . .

It was well past midnight when a tall, lean figure came striding along the edge of the highway that led past John's farm. In a pose Joanna would have recognised, he had his hands thrust deep in his pockets; his shoulders were hunched, his eyes trained on the surface of the road. He walked with a kind of underlying urgency, as if sheer physical activity, the covering of a certain number of miles, would keep the demons at bay. It was not the first time he had done this, walked himself into exhaustion so that he could sleep. Nor, he supposed wryly, glancing up at the farmhouse as he passed, would it be the last.

Then his steps slowed, and halted altogether. For the farmhouse was ablaze with lights, only a single one shining upstairs but nearly every window downstairs a yellow rectangle in the darkness. He frowned. The illuminated dial of his watch said one-thirty. Automatically his eyes searched the driveway, but there were only two cars parked there: John's battered one, Joanna's newer one. So it was not a party, not even a clandestine meeting with the handsome doctor.

Making a quick decision, Stephen turned up the driveway, walking in the wet grass at the edge of the gravel so that his approach was soundless. There was no other car behind the house, so he knew Joanna was alone. He did not want to frighten her. But on the other hand, and it was his city background speaking, she should not have gone to bed leaving all the lights on and the back door wide open. It was asking for trouble.

He tapped gently on the door. Misty was lying on her mat in the porch. She raised her elegant head, sniffed without much interest, and wagged her tail. As Stephen pulled the door open and stepped inside, she rolled over on her back, presenting her long-haired belly to be scratched.

Stephen clicked his tongue in mingled exasperation and amusement. John had mentioned once before how useless the collie was as a watchdog, but this was Stephen's first experience of Misty's welcoming attitude. 'Aren't you going to show me where the family silver's kept?' he muttered, obligingly rubbing her chest. 'Where's Joanna, Misty?' Thump, thump went the thick, caramel-coloured tail on the floor.

Stephen got to his feet and tapped on the connecting door between the porch and the kitchen. Faintly through the wood panels he could hear the sound of voices. When he pushed the door open, they were louder, accompanied by music, advising him that this particular brand of floor wax was easy to apply, absolutely non-yellowing, and during the entire month of May was reduced by thirty per cent. Magnificent savings! A bargain you couldn't afford to pass up. . . .

Stephen's brow cleared. Half prepared for what he

was going to see, he called softly, 'Joanna?' as he
walked across the kitchen and through the hall into the
living room. From the television screen an improbably
elegant housewife had just finished daintily applying the
floor wax to a tiled floor that was as shiny as an ice
rink. On the chesterfield Joanna was curled up, fast
asleep.

He smiled to himself, crossing the room so he could
turn the television off. In the sudden silence as the
picture shrank to a tiny dot on the screen he could hear
her breathing, quick, shallow breaths that made him
look at her more closely.

She was lying on her back, an eiderdown pulled up to
her waist, her cheek resting on one hand. Apart from a
hectic flush of colour on each cheekbone, her face was
paper-white. Damp tendrils of dark red hair clung to
her temples. Stephen reached out a hand, resting it
lightly on her forehead, almost ready for what he was
going to find: skin that was burning hot. Restlessly she
jerked her head away from his touch, muttering
something unintelligible under her breath.

Stephen took off his windbreaker, hanging it on a
chair, and knelt beside her. 'Joanna,' he said very
clearly. 'Joanna, wake up.' Her lashes flew up. Dazed
green eyes looked straight at him.

She was dreaming, Joanna thought in confusion, for
Stephen's face was only two feet from hers. She said,
stumbling a little on the words, 'I wish you really were
here,' and closed her eyes again.

'I am here—wake up!'

A hand was pressing her shoulder. She could not be
dreaming, it was too real, a firm, warm pressure that
dragged her back from the fever-bright images that had
been flickering across her brain. 'Stephen? Is it really
you?'

'Yes—I'm going to carry you up to bed, Joanna.'

'I think I'm ill,' she explained, somewhat redund-
antly.

'I think you are, too. Put your arms around my neck.'

Obediently she did as she was told, feeling his arms slide under her and lift her. The world lurched alarmingly, and with it, her stomach. She buried her face in his sweater. 'I feel lousy,' she quavered.

'You'll feel better when you're in bed. Do you have any aspirin?'

'Upstairs.' As he began mounting the staircase, each upward step seemed to jar her whole body, even though some tiny rational part of her brain knew he must be treading as softly as he could. She could hear what must be her own breathing, harsh, indrawn gasps that nevertheless did not quite seem to belong to her. Opening her eyes, she faltered, 'Let me off at the bathroom, please. Close the door.'

'All right. But call if you need me.'

He lowered her to her feet and somehow she managed to walk into the bathroom. She heard the latch click in place before she began to retch, her slim body convulsing in spasm after spasm. When there was nothing more to lose, she pulled herself upright, turning on the tap to rinse out her mouth and douse her face and hands, the shock of the cold water bringing her back to some semblance of normality.

'Joanna, are you all right? Can I come in?'

Swaying lightly on her feet, she opened the door herself. Each freckle stood out against the pallor of her face; there were bruised circles under her eyes, and she was frowning slightly, for his image had an alarming tendency to multiply itself until there were half a dozen Stephens standing there watching her. She sagged against his chest, needing to feel his solidity, to know in a nightmare world that he was real.

He lifted her again. 'Which is your room?'

'Across the hall.'

He edged the door open with his foot, so that light from the hall spilled into the room. It was a large room, not particularly tidy, but the accessories were brightly coloured, and something in the cheerful state of confusion of the books, the stuffed animals, the collection of seashells, spoke vividly of a love of life. For some reason it made Stephen smile.

Gently he lowered Joanna to the bed, pulling the covers back with his free hand; the sheets were flowered, the blanket a warm rose pink. 'I'll get you a drink of water, but I don't think we'll bother with the aspirin. Is there a glass in the bathroom?'

'Yes, by the medicine cabinet. There's a basin under the sink—maybe you'd better bring that, too.'

He seemed to be gone for a very long time, although actually it was less than a minute. Joanna was still sitting up in bed, and Stephen put an arm around her shoulders, holding out the glass. 'Here, you'd better have a drink.'

As he held the glass for her, his fingers curving over hers, his gentleness and concern brought tears of weakness to her eyes. 'I'm sorry. . . .' Her voice trailed off, because it seemed much too difficult to explain what she meant.

'You've nothing to be sorry for. Listen, Joanna, I'm going to stay here tonight—you shouldn't be alone with the boys. I'll sleep on the chesterfield. Call me if you need anything, okay?'

He had been edging the negligee off her shoulders as he spoke, putting it neatly across the foot of the bed. She blurted, 'You're getting involved, and you didn't want to.'

He was still sitting beside her on the bed, and briefly his eyes rested on her pale, worried face, and on the rounded smoothness of her arms and shoulders, bared by the nightdress. The dim light shadowed the hollow at her throat and the cleft between her breasts.

The grey eyes clouded over. 'I'll look after myself, Jo,' he said sombrely, and neither of them noticed how easily the diminutive of her name slipped from his tongue. 'Lie down now, and try and get some sleep.'

He leaned forward to adjust the bedcovers and in simple gratitude she pressed her lips to his cheek. His arms went around her, inexpressibly comforting. Burrowing her face into his shoulder, feeling the hardness of his collarbone against her cheek, she murmured drowsily, 'You smell nice.' With the suddenness of a tired child, she fell asleep in his arms.

He held her for several minutes, his face resting on her hair, until her breathing became deeper and more regular. Then he lowered her to the pillow, tucking the blankets around her. But even then he did not leave the room immediately. He sat quietly on the bed as the little clock on the night table ticked away the minutes, the old farmhouse surrounding him with the comfort and security of walls that had stood for so many nights in the past. His expression was unreadable, his dark eyes staring sightlessly at the floor.

When Joanna awoke the next day, she lay quite still under the covers, trying to sort out in her mind what had actually happened last night, and what she had dreamed. She had been ill, that much was certain. Although when she briefly touched her forehead it felt reassuringly cool, she was still aware of a great lassitude, a pervading weakness in her limbs that told her she was not fully recovered. Before her thoughts could carry her further, she looked over at the bedside clock, expecting it to say eight or perhaps even eight-thirty. The little gold hands stood at twenty past two. She blinked, looked again. The same. In a sudden panic she flung back the bedclothes and got out of bed. The boys . . . she had no idea where they were or how long they'd been up. Her heart dropped in her breast. What if something had happened to them? How would she ever explain to John?

On bare feet she ran out into the hall, seeing through their open door the unmade beds and the clutter of toys, hearing the silence that meant the room was empty. Maybe they were downstairs . . . grabbing at the rail, she raced down the stairs, with her other hand holding up the long folds of her nightgown. 'Brian!' she began to call, and then fell silent, pausing on the bottom step, her eyes glued to the figure sitting at the kitchen table as she remembered the rest of what had happened last night.

Stephen shoved back his chair, striding across the kitchen and into the hall. 'Joanna! What's wrong?'

Weak-kneed with relief, she sank down on the step. 'I woke up and saw the time, and got panic-stricken because of the boys—I'd forgotten you were here.' Briefly she rested her face against the newel post. 'I gave myself a real fright!'

'The boys are fine. They got up around eight, had their breakfast and went out to play. Home for lunch and back out again—no problems.'

She said guiltily, 'So you've been looking after them all day.'

'Precious little looking after is required, Joanna.'

'You didn't bargain for this when you moved in next door.'

With faint impatience he said, 'I don't think we need to discuss that right now. You'd better go up and get some clothes on, unless you want to add pneumonia to your troubles.'

It brought her to a jolting awareness of the scantiness of her attire, for the lace of the bodice cupped her breasts suggestively and the silky fabric clung to the lines of her body. She blushed a fiery red. 'I was so worried about the boys,' she said defensively. 'I didn't do it on purpose.' With a timing that completed her confusion, there clicked into her brain the statement Stephen had made to her in the back porch. I want to make love to you, Joanna, he had said, and now, as if he could not help himself, she saw his eyes linger on the curves of her body, hinted at yet not fully exposed by the softly draped nightgown.

Then he looked up, grey eyes meeting green like a jolt of electricity, for she had never seen such naked desire in a man's eyes. The breath caught in her throat. Strangely, instead of feeling embarrassment or constraint, she was aware of an uprush of pride. She was wanted; she was desirable. This dark-haired stranger who had voluntarily locked himself away from human contact found her, Joanna Hailey, to be a desirable woman. It was her first true intimation of her power as a woman, and because it was Stephen who had given her this knowledge, she felt her whole body respond to it, joyously, shamelessly, so that in her eyes was to be read the same message: I want you.

'You're very beautiful, Jo.'

The words were so softly spoken she had to strain to hear them, yet they scarcely needed to be said, for they were written in the unusual softness in his face. With a deliberate provocation she had not realised she was capable of, she allowed her gaze to slide from the peat-brown hair and the ruggedly carved face to the strong column of his throat, bared by his open-necked shirt, and the breadth of his shoulders. Dark hair curled on his chest. She would like to run her fingers through that hair, she thought with a wild, sweet ache of desire. She would like to slide her palms across the muscled hardness of his chest, savouring to the fullest the feel of a man's body, so compellingly different from her own.

Raising her eyes, her vivid face reflecting all the wonderment of new discoveries, she said, 'I've never felt this way with anyone before.' It had to be said, because by its very nature it was a revelation to be shared.

'I don't believe you have.'

Abruptly he turned away, so abruptly that she pulled herself to her feet. 'Stephen . . .?'

'It won't do, Joanna,' he said harshly, swinging round to face her again, the softness gone from his features, the barriers all in place. 'It just won't do. I don't know you very well, yet what I know I like and respect. That doesn't sound very romantic, but it happens to be true. But there can't be any kind of a relationship between us, particularly one that would include any—any physical closeness. I'll never marry again, Joanna, and I won't have an affair with you. Contrary to today's generalised image of men, I dislike casual affairs.'

Very quietly she said, 'I don't think an affair between you and me would be casual, Stephen.'

'You're right, of course—it wouldn't be. All the more reason that we stay clear of each other.'

'You're cutting off your nose to spite your face!'

'No, Jo, it's not that simple.' In a deliberate attempt to end the conversation, he said, 'Why don't you go and get your housecoat and I'll make you some toast and tea—I think you should eat something.'

Disconcertingly, because it seemed much too prosaic, she was aware of slight pangs of hunger. Knowing she was defeated before she spoke yet having to try, she said, 'I don't understand you, Stephen.'

'It's not necessary that you do. Once John gets back, I'll see very little of you.'

'Not if your horse is to be boarded here—you'll be over every day.'

'That's only a temporary arrangement. Joanna, I think you're in danger of exaggerating this whole thing. So the chemistry's right between us—so what? It doesn't mean we have to do anything about it. And it's nothing to do with that much maligned and over-used word love.'

She sat down again, clasping her knees, needing every ounce of her energy to do battle. For a battle it was, one in which her warmhearted, impetuous nature was pitted against a granite wall of obduracy, a withdrawal from love and laughter all the harder to comprehend because she could only guess at its sources. 'I don't know about that,' she said flatly. 'All I know is that I'm twenty-three years old, I've dated a fair number of different men, and until I met you, I'd never met one with whom I wanted to make love. There's something about you ... I don't know what it is or why it should be so, but there's something about you that's different from all the rest. And maybe I'm way off course, but I can't help thinking that I'm different for you, too—if that sounds conceited, I can't help it. Can't we give ourselves a chance, Stephen? Just keep on seeing each other, and see what happens?'

'No.'

She should have expected it, and it was, she supposed, a rejection she had asked for; but it hurt, nevertheless. Not wanting him to see the hurt, she took refuge in temper. 'You're determined to make a martyr of yourself, aren't you?' she blazed. 'You're in love with your own suffering!'

Stephen had been leaning against the doorframe. Now he straightened, taking three long steps towards her. 'That's not true,' he grated. 'How many times do I have to tell you that I'll never marry again, Joanna? You're a woman made for marriage. You should have a husband and children and a house of your own filled with love and laughter. I can't give you that. And I won't settle for half measures.'

He was standing close enough that she could have touched him, yet it was an illusion of closeness. How odd that he should have used her own phrase, she thought numbly ... love and laughter. Words that conjured up an image of felicity. But not for her. In a wave of weakness she knew she was defeated. 'I'm going upstairs,' she said stonily. 'I'll be down in a little while, and I'll get something to eat then.'

He nodded curtly. 'Very well.'

Joanna trailed up the stairs, hearing him go back into the kitchen as she took the first step. She was crazy, she thought bitterly. She had done it again—let her tongue run away with her, saying things that would have been better unsaid. And as a result, she had alienated

Stephen completely. Fools rush in where angels fear to tread . . . would she never learn?

Closing the door of her room, she went back to bed, determined to go over every word they had said and see where she had gone wrong. However, in spite of herself she fell asleep almost before she could get started, and when she woke again she could tell by the quality of light that it was early evening. From outside her door she heard a whispered consultation followed by a tentative tapping. 'Auntie Jo? Are you awake?'

She reached for her gown, quickly wrapping it around her shoulders. 'Come in!'

Mark opened the door, Brian following carrying a tray. 'We brought your supper,' Mark announced. 'Are you still sick?'

'I'm a lot better now,' she said cheerfully, knowing that their mother's long illness could not be far from their minds. 'Oh, Brian, it looks lovely!'

'I made the tea and the toast,' Brian told her. 'Stephen made the eggs—he said we could call him Stephen.'

'And I cut the cake,' Mark crowed.

Joanna smothered a smile, for the piece of sponge cake was far from square, and a large thumbprint adorned the icing. 'Thank you,' she said warmly. 'Have you had your supper?'

'We had chicken. Stephen made it—he's a good cook,' Mark said critically.

'He showed me how a car engine worked,' Brian added. 'He's a neat guy.'

There could be no higher praise. Not wanting to talk about Stephen any more, Joanna asked, 'What have you been doing all day?' The scrambled eggs were deliciously light and fluffy and she attacked them with gusto.

'We played in the sandpit and we went over to the Arsenaults—Lisette's got a new kitten. It's got a white face.'

The boys stayed until she had finished eating and then carried the tray downstairs. Joanna showered and washed her hair, putting on a long charcoal-grey woollen skirt and a plain white angora sweater, comfortable clothes for lounging in. She felt much better, the fever and nausea having gone, although the effort of drying her hair left her weak and tired. Taking a book from her shelves, she went downstairs.

Stephen and the boys were in the living room, the boys doing their homework, Stephen absorbed in some paperwork of his own. He looked up as she entered, a quick, comprehensive glance that took in the severely tailored skirt and the soft sweater, the crop of copper-coloured hair gleaming like fire under the overhead light. 'Feeling better?' he asked impersonally.

'Much, thank you,' she replied politely. 'And thank you for supper, it was delicious.' Curling up on the chesterfield, her feet tucked in the heavy folds of her skirt, she opened her book. Silence descended, broken only by Mark's heavy sighs as he wrestled with a handwriting exercise in his battered-looking workbook.

Determined that she should be no further indebted to Stephen, Joanna oversaw the boys' bedtimes, noting with a faint sense of jealousy, and then, dismayed by her own reaction, how warmly the two boys said goodnight to Stephen; they even persuaded him to read them a few pages of *Treasure Island* before they went upstairs, and he displayed an unexpected talent for mimicry, giving the villainous Long John Silver a bloodcurdling veracity.

As he put the book down despite cries for more, Joanna said drily, 'I hope we all won't have nightmares.'

'Nonsense,' he grinned. 'I'm sure children thrive on that stuff.'

How would you know? she asked herself silently. Did you have children of your own? He would be a good father, she decided, as he despatched the two upstairs with a firmness that brooked no arguments. She followed them up, making sure that their teeth were brushed and hands and faces washed before tucking them in. Then she went downstairs again, to find Stephen once again immersed in page after page of totally indecipherable equations. He had an air of permanence about him that made her chin lift rebelliously. 'There's no need for you to stay tonight, Stephen,' she said pleasantly. 'I feel much better now.'

'That's all right,' he said, not bothering to look up. 'I'd better stay, in case you have a relapse, or whatever. Besides, I don't like you being alone in this big house with the two boys and only that mutt of a dog to protect you.'

'She's not a mutt—she's a pure-bred collie!'

'You must be feeling better, you're starting to pick fights again!'

'Oh! You *are* exasperating!' She added nastily, 'You ought to go home, because the boys are starting to get fond of you, and that kind of thing doesn't fit into your scheme of the world, does it? Or are the children exempt?'

His jawline tightened fractionally, and the pencil being held in the lean, beautiful fingers suddenly snapped. There was a tiny, deadly silence.

Joanna whispered, 'I've said something wrong, haven't I?'

'Just leave it, Joanna. And it doesn't matter what you say, I'm staying tonight.' Stephen got up to sharpen the pencil, his back very eloquently turned towards her.

She picked up the book and stared sightlessly at the printed page. He must have had a child, she could think of no other explanation for his reaction. Would she never learn to guard her tongue? For despite his insistence on keeping her at arm's length, she had no desire to hurt him. The very opposite was true: she longed to be able to help him, to melt the ice in which he had encased a natural warmth and passion whose existence she would have sworn to on a stack of Bibles.

The minutes passed slowly. Stephen took out a pocket calculator and began to jot down some figures on a piece of paper, and eventually the book genuinely claimed Joanna's interest. However, at the end of a chapter she found her eyes leaving the page to look around at her surroundings, so very familiar yet subtly charged with a new clarity because of Stephen's presence. A stranger looking in would have seen a pleasant domestic scene, she thought with a catch in her breathing . . . the two young boys in bed, the man and woman sitting in companionable silence in the pleasantly shabby living room. Earlier Stephen had told her she should have a husband and children of her own; he was right, she thought numbly. But deep within her she was becoming more and more convinced that the man she wanted was the man she could not have: Stephen Moore. She understood neither how nor why it was happening, only that he seemed to be weaving himself into her thoughts and emotions in a way that frightened her, for she was powerless to resist it. She tried to tell herself that she was mistaken, that he was stubborn and cold and reserved to the point of rudeness, that she knew virtually nothing about his past, his family, his friends, his marriage. It made no difference. With a painful intensity her eyes lingered on his profile, on his faint frown of concentration and his thick, dark hair. Then, as if he sensed her appraisal, he looked up. 'What's the matter?'

Joanna could no more have stopped herself from blushing than she could have stopped breathing. 'Nothing,' she stammered. 'I—I guess I'll go up to bed now, Stephen, I'm tired.'

As she got to her feet, so too did he, and as though drawn by a magnet came to stand beside her. 'Don't worry about getting the boys off to school, I'll look after that . . . sleep well.'

'I hope you will, too.'

As if he could not help himself, he leaned forward. She waited, all of existence narrowing to a man's grey eyes, so close she felt herself lost in their depths. Then his lips brushed hers, the merest touch, a caress ended almost before it had begun. He stepped back, his face a taut mask, and she saw with a quiver of primitive excitement that he was breathing as hard as if he had been running. 'Go to bed, Joanna,' he said harshly. 'I'll see you in the morning.'

There was to be nothing more. The door had opened the merest chink and then had shut again. With a newfound wisdom Joanna did not fling herself against it to beat on its panels with her fists. She contented herself with saying softly, 'Goodnight, Stephen,' before she turned and left him. But she would remember that feather-light touch of his mouth on hers until the day she died, she thought fatalistically. Holding the memory of it to her now, as if it were a precious gem to be guarded, she went to bed and immediately fell into a profound and restful sleep.

CHAPTER FIVE

THE habits of many months die hard; Joanna was awake at six the next morning. She stayed in bed until Stephen, Brian, and Mark had all used the bathroom, then got dressed and went downstairs to the tantalising odour of bacon wafting from the kitchen. Stephen's casual, 'Good morning,' dispelled any romantic dreams she might have been clinging to; she busied herself preparing the boys' lunch pails, for they travelled to school on one of the big yellow school buses, and did not return until after three. The last-minute scurry for jackets and books was in full swing when from outside, cutting through the confusion, came the sound of child's sobbing. 'Who's that?' Joanna asked sharply, in the middle of zipping Mark's coat.

Brian ran to the window. 'It's Lisette—she's fallen down.'

Stephen headed for the back door, Joanna hard on his heels. As he went outside, she shoved her feet into her boots and went after him. He had not met Lisette before, but something in his manner must have allayed the child's fear of strangers; as Joanna rounded the corner of the house, she saw him kneeling beside the little girl and then effortlessly lifting her in his arms. 'Joanna's here,' he was saying. 'We'll wash it off and put a bandage on it for you.'

Feeling rather redundant, Joanna followed the pair of them back into the kitchen, where Lisette gave Mark a watery grin as Stephen perched her on the edge of the table. 'I tripped,' she hiccupped.

She had torn one leg of her cotton slacks; Stephen carefully pushed the material up over her knee, baring a nasty graze ingrained with dirt. Lisette's face puckered at the sight of it. 'It hurts,' she whimpered.

70

'I'm sure it does,' Stephen replied gently. 'Jo, get some warm water and a cloth, will you?'

He had taken control so naturally that Joanna did as he asked without questioning, fetching disinfectant and some sterile pads as well. Then she shooed the boys, who would much rather have stayed and watched, out of the back door. 'Off you go, or you'll miss the bus.'

'So will Lisette.'

'We'll have to run her home to change her trousers before she can go to school. Look, there comes the bus—run!'

The two boys raced down the driveway, lunch pails banging against their knees, jackets flapping. Joanna watched until they were safely on board, waving goodbye as she knew John or Sally always did, before going back into the house. The clean-up was proceeding slowly, Stephen taking infinite care to hurt as little as possible, his big hands both deft and gentle. Although Lisette was keeping a close eye on the proceedings, she was also chattering away about the new kitten with the white face, Stephen putting in a question now and then to keep her going. Finally he straightened. 'I think that's got all the dirt out. We'll put some ointment and a nice white bandage on it and then we'll run you home.'

'Okay. Then you can meet the kitten. Its name is Buffoon.'

Joanna went to get a sweater and her car keys. As she came back in the kitchen, Stephen had just finished taping the end of the bandage, a neat job Drew could hardly have bettered. He eased the trouser leg down over the child's knee. 'There—all set. Let's go and meet Buffoon.'

The child giggled up at him entrancingly, a dimple appearing in each plump cheek. 'Buffoon!' With the unselfconsciousness of the very young, she raised her arms so Stephen could pick her up, her dancing brown eyes belying the tearstains on her face.

Stephen had been reaching out for her, a smile on his own face. But as thought a film had been stopped at a particular frame so the characters were frozen in their poses, he was suddenly transfixed, his hands encircling the child's fragile ribcage, his face only inches from hers. The smile vanished from his eyes, engulfed as if it had never been by a wave of such naked agony that it was all Joanna could do not to cry out. His teeth were clenched, the muscles standing out like ropes in his neck.

Whether it was Lisette's whimper of fear or Joanna's croaked, 'Stephen?' that brought him back to his senses, she never knew. She saw him gulp in air as if he had been choking; give his head a shake as though to dispel some nightmare image; and by a superhuman effort produce what could have passed as a smile. 'Sorry, Lisette,' he whispered, and Joanna would have sworn he had forgotten there was anyone else in the room. 'You—reminded me of someone.' His smile was a little more convincing. 'Are you ready to go?'

Still subdued, the child nevertheless trustingly buried her head in Stephen's shoulder as he picked her up. Briefly his eyes closed as his lips rested on her hair. Then he raised his head, his features rinsed of all expression, blank as a death mask. 'All set, Jo?'

She had been clutching the back of the chair so hard she could feel the strain all the way up her wrists. Hoping her voice would sound normal, she said, 'We'll take my car.'

The three of them went out of the back door into the spring morning. From the woods echoed a chorus of birdsong, trills, cheeps, and whistles, like the unco-ordinated tuning up of an orchestra. The buds were fat on the trees, while against the house the crocuses had opened their gold-centred flowers to the sun.

Still shaken by what she had just witnessed, Joanna started the car and turned around in front of the barn. It was a matter of minutes to reach the Arsenault property, their house newly painted in yellow and white, their fields already ploughed. As Stephen held Lisette, Joanna tapped on the door. Della opened the door, plump, bustling Della with the sharp tongue and the heart of gold. 'It's all right,' Joanna said quickly. 'She fell and hurt her knee—nothing serious.'

Stephen relinquished Lisette to Della's massive bosom. 'If I've told you once I've told you a dozen times not to run everywhere, Lisette! Walking gets you there just the same.' She clicked her tongue. 'And your new slacks—a big hole! I'll get your red ones, you'll have to wear those today. In the meantime you'd better have a cookie and a glass of milk.'

Della had raised five strapping sons on this mixture of vinegar and sugar, and Joanna had no doubt Lisette received less of the vinegar and more of the sugar than any of the boys. 'Would you like me to drive her to school, Della?' she asked. 'I don't have to go to work today. By the way, this is our new neighbour, Stephen Moore—he bandaged Lisette's knee. Stephen, Della Arsenault.'

Della acknowledged the introduction briskly. 'Thank you for your help, Mr Moore. No, no, Joanna, Léon will take her.' Léon was her husband, a stocky Acadian who could trace his ancestors on the Island back to the early seventeen-hundreds, and whose slow, methodical manner no longer deceived Joanna, for it was the old story of the turtle and the hare: he could accomplish more in a day than another man in two.

'Are you sure?'

'Oh yes, he has lots of time. Will you both stay for a cup of tea?'

'We'd better get back.' Stephen favoured Della with his rare smile, to which Della was no more immune than was she herself, Joanna noticed with amusement. 'I have to meet John today and I should get an early start. Another time.'

Forgetting her sore knee, Lisette scrambled to the

floor and hauled the white-faced kitten out from behind the stove; Stephen duly admired it, and then to a round of thanks and goodbyes he and Joanna left. 'Why don't you take me straight to my house?' he suggested. 'I should leave as soon as possible.'

Wondering how she was going to phrase what needed to be said, Joanna negotiated the Arsenaults' steep driveway, then drove the half mile or so to Stephen's. Over the years the Wintons had spared no expense: the curving lane that led up to the house through the trees was paved, flanked at its entrance by stone pillars and a wrought iron fence. The house itself was built in Georgian style of mellow grey-toned brick, black shutters on the square-paned windows, the slate roof shaded by tall elms and maples. Sprinkled among the trees, the daffodils were just coming into bloom. Joanna gave an unconscious sigh of pleasure. 'It's a beautiful house. So welcoming, somehow.'

As if to deny her words, he did not invite her in. 'I'm going to have to find someone to look after the grounds. You mentioned the Arsenault boys—maybe one of them would do it.'

Was that why he had been so friendly to Della, because he wanted something from her? Surely not ... but he had given her the opening she wanted. 'Stephen, what happened in the kitchen when you picked up Lisette? For a few moments you looked just terrible.'

He said flatly, reaching for the doorhandle, 'It was nothing.'

She put her hand on his sleeve, feeling the roughness of his sweater under her fingers. 'It was much more than nothing.'

'Leave it, Joanna.'

'You had a daughter, didn't you?' she persisted. 'Lisette reminded you of her.'

He jerked his arm free, his face convulsed with anger. 'The past is dead, Joanna. I don't want you or anyone else dragging it all out into the open again—do you understand?'

'Is she dead?'

The question hung in the air between them. Like two stones, his eyes stared at her dispassionately. He said with a clarity and lack of emotion that must have been deliberate, 'I have no idea whether she is alive or dead.'

As appalled as he had meant her to be, Joanna watched in silence as he got out of the car, slammed the door, and strode across the courtyard to the wide front door. Unlocking it, he disappeared inside without a backward look.

She was shaking, horribly near tears. She had to get out of here before she began to cry like a baby. Round the oval rose garden and down the lane again, along the highway to the farmhouse: the journey seemed to take for ever. She parked the car by the house, from pure habit gave Misty an absentminded pat on the nose, and went inside. The basin and the roll of bandage were still sitting on the pine table. Sinking into a chair, Joanna rested her elbows on the table and buried her face in her hands.

When Joanna got up fifteen minutes later, she had done some very hard thinking, and it had all led to one inevitable conclusion: she must leave Stephen Moore alone, somehow forget that he even existed. Over and over again he had ordered her to do just that, and she had blithely ignored him, convinced that somehow she could help him, bring him back to life, make him whole again. Just call me Pollyanna, she thought bitterly. But after today she could no longer ignore his strictures. His sorrows were not her sorrows, his private demons nothing to do with her. And her own growing conviction that he was the one man she had been waiting for all her life she must somehow subdue. Thank God she had shared it with no one else.

Listlessly she got up from the table and began to tidy

the kitchen, her quite automatic actions unfortunately leaving her mind free. She was just an ordinary girl, she knew. She had had loving parents, a happy childhood, an older brother to adore; she had spent two years at a technological institute in Halifax, but apart from that she had lived all her life on the Island and had been content to do so. It didn't add up to very much. Ordinary really was the word to describe it. But Stephen Moore was not like that. His sophistication, self-confidence, and formidable intelligence were so integral a part of him that he took them for granted; he was different from her, not even remotely a part of her world, and the sooner she faced up to that the better. He was introverted where she was outgoing, cold where she was passionate, detached where she was involved. He was not for her. . . .

She realised she was still scrubbing at the same patch on the counter long after it was spotless. With an actual effort of will she forced all thought of Stephen to the very back of her mind and began to plan her day. John would probably be home for dinner—but would he bring Stephen with him? Oh, damn . . . she was going to have to do better than that. She would make a big pot of fish chowder for supper, with cheese biscuits and a deep dish apple pie, all of John's favourites; he would probably be feeling depressed after leaving Sally. She would clean his room and run the vacuum over the rest of the house. And she'd pick some forsythia and pussy willows to brighten up the hall. What she was not going to do was sit around and mope all day.

A praiseworthy ambition, and one she did her best to fulfil. Although she could still feel the after-effects of her bout of illness, which coupled with emotional strain had a tendency to slow her down, by the time the boys came home the house looked clean and tidy, and the chowder was simmering on the stove. She fed them about six, cleaned up the dishes, changed into a flared moss-green skirt and tailored blouse, and sat down to wait. It was nearly nine when she heard the sound of tyres in the driveway. Protestingly, the boys had gone to bed half an hour earlier. Now she heard the thud of footsteps racing down the stairs. 'Dad's home!' Mark yelled, but it was Brian who beat him into the kitchen and was the first to catapult into his father's arms. John hugged both his sons, attempting to answer all their excited questions, then producing letters from their mother. Only then did he give Joanna a hug, kissing her on the cheek. 'I hear you were ill on Saturday,' he said pointedly. 'Did you know you were coming down with something before I left?'

Her smile was demure. 'How can you suggest such a thing?'

'You knew I wouldn't have gone if I'd realised you were ill.'

'Right on.'

He gave her a little shake. 'You're hopeless, Jo! You still look a bit peaked.'

Very much aware of Stephen standing silently listening, she changed the subject. 'How's Sally?'

His face brightened. 'Much better than I'd expected. She's up walking a couple of times a day—she uses one of those metal supports, but at least she can do it. I had a long chat with the surgeon, and he thinks she may be home in three weeks.'

'Oh John, that would be wonderful! I do hope so.'

'So do I,' said John, a masterly understatement if Joanna had ever heard one. 'Do I smell chowder? I'm starving—we didn't stop to eat because we were later than we'd expected. Pull up a chair, Stephen.'

'I won't——'

'Yes, you will,' John interrupted ruthlessly. 'The least we can do is feed you after all you've done for us.'

Quickly Joanna laid two places at the table, and John and Stephen began to eat, the boys listening wide-eyed as their father filled in the details of his weekend and gave them more news of their mother. Then he shooed them upstairs. 'Clean your teeth. I'll be right up.' Turning to Stephen, he said, 'I want to spend a few minutes with them before they go to sleep—Sally had messages for both of them. By all means stay if you want to, Stephen. But in case you leave before I come down . . .' He held out his hand, his face very grave. 'It meant a lot to me and Sally that we could see each other this weekend—thanks. That's really all I can say.'

The two men clasped hands and then John left the room. Stephen bent to pick up his jacket. 'Thank you for the meal, Joanna.'

She had expected him to rush out of the door the moment John was gone. But instead he stood there holding his jacket, looking down at her as though he expected her to say something. It seemed a very long time since the morning and his precipitate leaving of her. She said uncertainly, 'Did you have a good flight?'

'It was fine, no problems. The reason we were so late was because I went to the hospital from the airport—I didn't want to turn around and fly straight back.'

'Oh . . . did you meet Sally?'

'Yes. I liked her. Although I couldn't place the absolute trust in another person that they do in each other.'

In silence Joanna began to pick up the dirty dishes, stacking them on the counter. Earlier today she had made a vow to herself, and this was the first testing point. No more arguments with him, no more involvement. Avoiding looking in his direction, wishing he would leave, she rinsed off the bowls.

'Could you?'

Back to him, she said with calculated uninterest, 'I suppose I could if I loved the person.' She turned the taps on full blast, hoping that would give him the hint.

'Here, why don't I help you with those? John's right, you do still look tired.'

'I can manage, thank you.'

'I'm sure you can.' There was an odd note in his voice. 'But that's not the point.'

'The point is that I'd rather do them alone,' she replied tersely.

As if she had not spoken, he put his jacket down and picked up a dish towel. 'They do love each other, don't they?' he said slowly, as though thinking aloud. 'On the way up on Saturday John looked like a kid on his way to a Christmas party. Then today, when it was time to leave the hospital, I went out of the room so they could be alone to say goodbye. John came out looking like he'd just had a limb amputated. He chainsmoked all the way to the airport before he said a word to me. What if something happened to one of them, Joanna? The other would never survive.'

'You're wrong.' She immersed her hands in the suds and began to wash the dishes with frenetic energy.

'How so?'

Her hands stilled as she turned to face him. 'Look, Stephen, I wish you'd just go home and keep out of my life. This morning you couldn't wait to be rid of me, and now you won't leave me alone.' She added jaggedly, 'How am I supposed to know what to say or do? You keep changing the rules.'

'This morning I was—upset.'

'So you do have emotions.'

'You know damn well I do!'

Danger in the edge to his voice. . . . 'Then act upon them,' she said recklessly, forgetting all her fine resolutions.

'I did that once, Joanna. And it was a total and unmitigated disaster from which I've never fully escaped.'

'Your marriage, you mean?'

'That, and other things. Now answer my question— what would happen if either John or Sally were to die?'

'The one who was left would manage somehow. Would do more than that—in time would be grateful for all they had shared together, glad to have had it.' She hesitated, knowing she was putting into words a deeply felt but never before expressed conviction. 'There's risk in nearly everything, and no guarantees anywhere. So does one never love anyone in case something should happen to that person? That's no way to live—you might as well be dead yourself.'

'And do you really believe marriages can last?'

'Of course they can. But they don't just happen—both partners have to give a lot of themselves. It's when you see a couple like John and Sally that you know it's worth it. What's between them is virtually indestructible.'

With a strange gentleness in his voice, he said, 'I hope you never get disillusioned, Jo.'

She looked at him, her green eyes troubled. 'As you have been.'

'Some day, maybe, I'll tell you about it.' As if he could not help himself, he reached out and laid his hand on her shoulder, where it lay, warm and heavy.

She felt the contact through every nerve in her body and unconsciously she swayed towards him. 'Have you ever told anyone?'

'Never.' With the ball of his thumb he was stroking her flesh through the thin material of her shirt, a hypnotic caress that made her ache for more. His eyes trained on her face, he said heavily, 'You seem so honest and true, Joanna, so real—but then so did she.'

'What was her name?'

'Laura. She was the most beautiful woman I've ever seen.'

A stab of pure jealousy ripped through the girl, for there was a note in his voice she had never heard before. Suddenly hating the conversation, she pulled away, so that his hands fell to his side. Turning away, head downbent, she whispered, 'What do you want of me, Stephen?'

'I wish to God I knew, Joanna. On the one hand I'm pulled to you—God, how I'm pulled to you! Yet on the other hand, there's a voice in me screaming a warning, saying you got caught once, don't do it again.' She felt his fingers stroking the nape of her neck where the chestnut curls clustered, and trembled at his touch. 'When I'm as near to you as this, I hardly hear the voice,' he said deliberately.

She knew she had only to turn her head and he would kiss her, knew it in her bones. And she, who had never been afraid of a man in her life, was afraid to do so, for intuitively she sensed that while Stephen could bring her happiness such as she had never dreamed of, he could also cause her to suffer, suffer terribly. Because she had never learned to prevaricate, she muttered, 'I'm afraid of you.'

The fingers stilled, then were gone. She sensed, rather than saw, him move away from her. 'That's probably very wise of you,' he said drily, and she knew their brief intimacy was over. Forcing herself not to think, she finished washing the cutlery as quickly as she could; when John came back downstairs the kitchen was tidy and Stephen had just left, his curt goodnight still echoing in her ears.

'You'd better go to bed, Sis,' said John, concerned. 'You look beat.'

'I am, I guess. I'm glad you got away, though.'

He grinned boyishly. 'Me, too . . . what shift are you on tomorrow?'

'Three to eleven all this week. So I'll sleep at the apartment and come out here a couple of mornings to do some baking and cleaning.'

'All right—but don't overdo it, Jo. The boys will survive on cookies bought at the store for once.'

'I'm sure they would . . . I suppose I'm trying as much as possible to do all the things Sally does.'

'I know you are, Jo—you're a dear. Off to bed with you, now. And I'll get the boys off to school tomorrow while you sleep in—that's an order!' As he slapped her on the bottom, she fled, laughing. At least John appreciated her. That, and the boys' affection, she could count on. As for Stephen, her relationship with him was like the sand on the beach, she thought fancifully, always shifting, never the same two days in a row. A house built on sand. . . .

CHAPTER SIX

MAY had slipped imperceptibly into June. The sun's warmth was more convincing, while the first delicate green leaves were unfurling from the buds on the trees. At the farm the tulips and daffodils paraded their vivid hues, and the heifers gambolled in the fields, intoxicated by the fresh green grass and the vagrant breezes that blew from the blossom-laden orchards. Joanna spent three mornings at the farm during the week, for she had never been able to resist the apple blossoms; the orchard was like a sea of pink, the air sweetly scented and pregnant with the buzzing of bees. Yet somehow this year the magic was not quite the same. All the time she was there she was naggingly conscious of Stephen's proximity, so near and yet so far. She did not see him all week. It was almost as if he knew when she would be there and was staying away.

On the Tuesday afternoon when she had been at work, his horse Rajah had finally been delivered, to be housed in the stall next to Star's. The first chance she got Joanna went up to inspect him. As she had expected, he was a magnificent creature, a black stallion two hands higher than Star, glossy of coat and proud of mien. She was careful to give Star her full share of attention, but she had brought an extra carrot for the stallion. He took it from her delicately, his lips velvet-soft on her palm, and despite his fiery temperament she was sure there was not a vicious bone in his body. She wondered, without much hope, if she would ever be given the chance to ride him.

On Saturday she switched back to the early shift, and on Saturday evening, rather against her better judgement, she had agreed to go out with Drew; she had seen

83

little of him lately, since he spent the mornings at the hospital and the afternoons at his private practice, so their schedules had not coincided. It seemed like an effort to get ready; she could not help realising how different she would feel were she preparing for a date with Stephen. Not that she had ever formally gone out with him, she thought miserably. No chance of that.

They went to the seven o'clock showing of a film that had received a couple of awards. Mistakenly, Joanna decided, for she found the plot and the dialogue equally unconvincing, although the photography was magnificent. On the way to their usual restaurant she and Drew argued amicably about it, and once there ordered a drink while they were waiting for their meal. 'So what have you been up to lately, Joanna?' Drew asked. 'You don't look to me as though you're fully over that bout of 'flu you had last week.'

She felt a flash of irritation. She was tired of people telling her she looked tired. 'Nothing much, really. Same old routine.' Absently she rearranged the cutlery in a straight row, lining up the tines of the forks.

'What's wrong?'

Suddenly ashamed of herself, she gave him her full attention. '*I* don't know, Drew—spring fever, maybe.' She smiled ruefully. 'Have you got the cure for that?'

He grinned back. 'It's not in the medical books. I've said it before and I'll say it again—I'll be damn glad when Sally's back home and you can get the benefit of your time off. You're doing too much, honey.'

Not for the first time it occurred to her that 'honey' was not one of her favourite endearments. 'It's not that, Drew—I'm glad to be able to help out.'

'Then what is it?' He hesitated, his handsome face looking uncharacteristically unsure of itself. 'You've mentioned this new neighbour once or twice. Stephen, is that his name? Is it something to do with him?'

The sudden drop of her lashes to hide her expression

was a dead giveaway. To give herself time, she murmured, 'Why do you ask that?'

'Because you're not yourself, Joanna.' There was unusual forcefulness in his voice.

She raised her eyes. They had been friends for a long time, she and Drew, and he deserved the truth. 'You're right, it is to do with him. Everything seems to have changed since he arrived, yet if you were to ask me why, I don't know if I could answer. I'm not in love with him—how could I be? And he's certainly not in love with me. But he disturbs me. He's different from anyone else I've ever met, and he makes me feel different.' The waiter came with their entrée, and she paused until he had gone. 'I know that probably doesn't make much sense to you, Drew—it doesn't make much sense to me either. But it's all I can tell you.'

'I see,' he said heavily. 'I was afraid it might be something like that.'

She abandoned any pretence of interest in her food. 'Afraid?'

'There's no chance you could be even a bit in love with me, is there, Joanna?'

'Oh, Drew. . . .'

'I can tell by your face that there isn't.' He made an attempt at a smile. 'Don't look so worried. I should have said something a month or more ago, but I thought you needed more time, and then things got so hellish busy at the hospital.' In one of his rare flashes of humour he added, 'The classic doctor's excuse.'

'You mean . . .?'

'I was working up to asking you to marry me.'

She reached across the table and rested her hand on his. 'That's sweet of you, Drew, really it is. But I can't . . . you know that, don't you? There's no gentle way of saying it, but I'm just not in love with you. That's got nothing to do with Stephen—it's simply the way it is.'

'Do you think it will change?'

She could not be less than honest. 'No, I don't.'

Rather aimlessly he picked up his fork and poked at his food. 'Then that's that.'

'I'm sorry,' she said helplessly.

He produced the semblance of a smile. 'It's not your fault. As you say, it's just the way things are.'

They began to eat, Drew changing the subject to an exhibition of paintings he had seen at the Confederation Centre Gallery the week before. But for neither of them could the remainder of the evening be called a success. By a kind of mutual consent they skipped dessert, and Drew drove Joanna straight home to her apartment. Keeping very much to his side of the car seat, he said, 'Let's still get together for a coffee or a movie sometimes, Joanna. After all, we'll be seeing each other at the hospital every day.'

'Yes. . . .' The last thing she wanted was for either of them to become the subject of gossip at the hospital, and she knew Drew's suggestion was a sensible one. 'You're a good friend, Drew,' she said impulsively.

'Yeah . . . well, that's something, anyway. Goodnight, Joanna.'

'Goodnight.'

She let herself into the apartment and closed the door behind her with a sigh of relief, glad to be alone. There was no other way she could have handled the situation, but even so she did not feel particularly good about it, for Drew had been hurt, she knew.

Undressing slowly, she got into bed, purposely trying to forget the evening and think instead of the farm, when tomorrow she could ride Star through the orchard, and fill the house with daffodils. And maybe, just maybe, see Stephen. . . .

She did not see Stephen. Everything else should have been perfect: it was a crisp, sunny day, the apple trees were a vision of delight, and the boys were flatteringly pleased to see her. She raced through the chores, certain that Stephen would want to ride Rajah in the afternoon. Perhaps they could go together ... but by four o'clock, she could wait no longer. She called Star from the pasture where the two horses were peacefully grazing, saddled her, and rode through the woods that belonged to the Arsenaults to the eastern shore of the bay; far to her left was the beach that belonged to Stephen, where she had thrown the stick for Misty on an early morning in April. Five weeks ago, she calculated, counting backwards over the days. In some ways it seemed like for ever, in others only yesterday.

The turquoise waters of the bay danced and sparkled in the sunlight. Joanna led Star across the dunes where the eel grass whipped around the mare's fetlocks and the purple flowers of the beach pea nodded in the sea wind. The air was crisp and clean and invigorating, and when they reached the long curve of the beach, Joanna urged Star into a canter.

At the end of the beach was an island that could be reached only at low tide, for dangerous currents surged around it and its shoreline was never the same two weeks in a row. Today the tide was coming in; in the channel that separated the island from the mainland the water eddied and swirled and the waves clashed. Joanna pulled the horse up. The island had intrigued her for as long as she could remember, in its inaccessibility so much of the time and its constant state of change. But today she would have to content herself with looking at it, for the water was too deep to risk forging the channel. Regretfully she turned Star homewards.

Perhaps subconsciously she had been hoping to meet Stephen on her ride. But there was no sign of him, and when she arrived home Rajah was still munching the grass in the pasture. Determined that his absence was not going to ruin her day, she rubbed Star down, had a quick shower, and prepared dinner, sending one of the boys to get John from the lower field where he was seeding. Dishes, homework to be supervised, ironing: she drove herself from one job to the next, thoroughly out of sorts but convinced she was hiding it in a flurry of activity. Finally John said mildly, 'Relax, Sis. You've got tomorrow off, haven't you? You don't have to do it all today.'

He knew her much too well. 'I'm not in the mood for relaxing,' she retorted, adding with no great originality, 'I'm as restless as—as a cat on a hot tin roof.'

The look he gave her was both affectionate and shrewd, although all he said was, 'Then go out for a walk. It's a lovely evening and the moon's just coming up.'

'Maybe I will ... sorry, John, I'm not very good company.' She hesitated. 'Drew asked me to marry him last night.'

'I see. I would gather you said no.'

'Mmm. He's nice, and I'm fond of him, but I don't love him.'

'I never really thought he was the right one for you.'

'Didn't you? I didn't know that.'

'I figured you'd find it out for yourself sooner or later.'

Knowing that if she stood here much longer she'd be confiding all her confusion about Stephen, and for some reason chary of doing that, she gave him a false, bright smile. 'I'm going to take your advice—don't wait up for me.'

Running upstairs she changed into dark slacks and a black turtleneck sweater, for the nights were still cool. Sneakers on her feet, her navy windbreaker over her head, and she was ready. Leaving the house a few minutes later, she started up towards the barn. It felt better to be outdoors, the night's looming shadows suiting her mood more than the kitchen's cosy domesticity. Without conscious decision she headed for the orchard.

It was not quite fully dark. The blossoms were dulled to a ghostly grey, the black trunks in straight rows like soldiers on parade. Overhead the first stars shone, cold, infinitely distant. Joanna began to walk faster, shoving her hands in the pockets of her windbreaker. By the time she reached the hay field the white arc of the moon had risen over the tops of the trees behind her, casting an illusory light into the woods. Stephen's woods. Damn him anyway, she thought. She knew those woods like the back of her hand, had played hide and seek in them and climbed the trees. Why should she stay out of them now just because he said so?

Instead of heading down to the shore, she began to work her way uphill, more in the direction of the house. There was a narrow trail leading through the woods, which she followed until the trees began to thin out; through the network of branches, still not fully in leaf, she saw the yellow glow of lights from the house. She wished she had the courage to walk up to it and knock on the door, and knew she did not. Pulling up her hood, because it was cold, she stood still for a few minutes, then began to work her way a little closer, making no particular effort to be quiet.

The moon was fully over the horizon now, casting an eerie half-light over the trees, their shadows like many-fingered hands on the grass. From down by the shore a barred owl called, hoohoo hoohoo . . . hoohoo hoohoo, while from behind the orchard another one hooted a reply. Joanna moved between the trees, now in the moonlight, now in shadow, a skulking black-clad figure made anonymous by the night.

She had no inkling that she was not alone. Her senses, lulled by the security of long-familiar surroundings, gave her no warning. She was emerging from a copse of alders, her head ducked to avoid the branches poking at her face, when she was seized by one arm, pulled off balance and flung against a tree trunk, a hand at her throat choking off her instinctive scream. Unable to breathe, a branch digging cruelly into her back, she made a tiny whimper of protest.

Her hood had fallen back, and the moon's pale

radiance fell across her face with its shocked, wide-held eyes and parted lips. The hand clamped about her neck loosened its hold. She drew a deep, shaking breath as Stephen exclaimed, 'Joanna! What the hell are you doing out here?' She pushed herself away from the trunk, rubbing at her back, unable to say a word. Her heart was racing as though she had run a mile. He was very close to her, his face harshly shadowed, and when he spoke again she knew he was as shaken as she. 'God! Are you all right?' She nodded, still speechless. 'You little idiot—I could have really hurt you! I was out on the back verandah, saw you coming and figured you were a thief—that's what comes of living too long in the city. Thought I'd get you before you got me.'

'You did,' she croaked, resting her fingers on her neck with a reminiscent shudder.

As if he could not help himself, Stephen let go of her arm, brought both hands up to cup her face, and lowered his head to hers. Far away in the woods the owl hooted again, but neither of them heard it.

This kiss was very different from the other one. This time, the moment his lips touched hers, they were both lost. She was crushed against him as his mouth branded its mark on her, never still, learning every detail of the softness of her lips. The stars plummeted in the sky as his mouth made its own demand. She opened to him, joyously, generously, until there was nothing in the world but a kiss that she wanted to last for ever.

When he did, finally, raise his head, she must have made a tiny moan of protest. Her hands, she discovered, were clasping his shoulders; her body was so closely pressed against him that even through their clothing she felt, with a wild leap of her blood, how aroused he was. Dazedly she knew that here in his arms was where she wanted to be. As if he had read her mind, he rasped, 'I've been wanting to do that since the first moment I saw you.'

His second kiss was more gentle, with a deliberate

sensuality that made her head swim; he nibbled at her lips, sliding his mouth over hers, until she thought she would faint with the pleasure of it. She whispered shakily, 'Oh, Stephen . . . I've never been kissed like this before. Never felt anything like it.' She clutched at his shoulders for support, feeling with a primitive thrill the hardness of bone and muscle under his sweater. 'Why? Why should it be you that makes me feel this way?'

'Why is it you who's making me forget all the promises I made to myself?' He shook his head. 'I don't know, Joanna . . . I don't have any of the answers. I only know I don't want to fight it any more.'

Through the trees the owl hooted again, so far away that it was a ghostly repetition of its earlier call. Then from nearby they heard the heavy beat of wings and the thin scream of some tiny creature caught in the bird's talons. Joanna shivered, her brain telling her it was all part of the nature of things, her emotions somehow seeing the swift, nocturnal death as a bad omen.

More normally, Stephen said, 'You're cold. Let's go in, and I'll make you a drink.'

Also trying to school her voice to normality, she replied, 'That would be lovely.'

He took her hand, leading her towards the back of the house. The tall glass doors on the verandah were not locked; sliding them open, he ushered her indoors. Joanna had not been inside the house since last summer when the Wintons had been in residence; Emily Winton had once visited Britain and had fallen in love with some of the stately homes of England, as a consequence of which her house on the Island had been overstuffed with imitations of Sheraton and Hepplewhite furniture, as well as chandeliers, fake marble fireplaces, dark family portraits and ornately fringed draperies. All of this was gone now, Joanna saw as Stephen led her from the library through the hall to the living room; the rooms had been restored to a simplicity that allowed their beautiful proportions to speak for themselves. In the living room, which faced the front of the house, a fire glowed in the brick hearth. She was not well versed in interior decorating, but even to her uneducated eyes the furniture looked plain, expensive and good, the colours harmonious, the whole effect one of quality and comfort. It was, however, undeniably a man's room. She said spontaneously, 'You should have a bowl of daffodils on that table—a pewter bowl, preferably. It would look lovely against the panelling.'

He said ironically, 'The woman's touch.' Joanna blushed, going to kneel by the fire so she need not look at him, holding out her hands to the blaze. He threw on another log. 'What would you like to drink?'

'A rum and coke—I have plebeian tastes.'

He chuckled. 'I'll be right back.'

While he was gone, Joanna stared into the pulsing heart of the flames, her body very still. Over the past half hour her whole life had changed irrevocably, she knew. Never again would she be the innocent girl, waiting for she knew not what; two kisses had changed her into a woman, with a woman's knowledge of her power to arouse and equally a woman's knowledge of her own needs. She wanted Stephen Moore, she thought, her cheeks flushed from more than the heat of the fire. Wanted him in the most direct and primitive way possible. Her brow furrowed. But she wanted more than that. She wanted the whole man, his thoughts and emotions, his laughter and sadness, his past and his present . . . and his future.

'What are you thinking?'

She jumped, because she had not heard him come back. He sank down on the carpet beside her, holding out a glass. 'Cheers.'

She raised it to her lips and took a cautious sip. 'I'll have to make that last,' she said primly. 'I have no head for alcohol at all.'

'You didn't answer my question.'

'I don't know how to answer it.' She looked straight

at him, her eyes darkened by the stark black of her sweater. 'Maybe it's your turn to answer a few questions, Stephen—after all, I know virtually nothing about you.'

'I could say the same of you.'

He was fencing with her, keeping her at a distance. 'Oh, there's nothing much to tell about me,' she said impatiently. 'It's all very ordinary. Loving parents, a happy childhood, the ordinary pains of adolescence. Dates, dances, a job. What else is there to say? But I don't think things have been that simple for you. Or that commonplace. For one thing——' pointedly she looked around the understated luxury of the room, 'you must be rich.' She made it sound almost like a crime.

'Inherited, Joanna. Does that make it better or worse?'

With the air of one making a discovery, she said, 'I don't think you're used to talking about yourself, are you? Has there never been anyone to listen?'

He stared moodily into the flames. 'I suppose there hasn't been. My father was always too busy making money, my mother spending it. I was their only child, relegated to a series of different private schools because we were always moving. So I would just start to make friends and it would be time to go again. Move on to the next place to make the next million.' His voice was bitter. 'By the time I was a teenager the pattern had been set—I was a loner, an outsider. I can't imagine that you were like that, Jo.'

Her smile had a tinge of self-mockery. 'Afraid not. I was usually smack in the middle of whatever was going on. . . . But you've learned to make friends since then.'

'Oh, yes. But if you're to understand my marriage, you have to understand what I was like then. The next crisis was my choice of career. My father wanted me to be a lawyer, so I could help him with all the behind-the-scenes legalities—and illegalities—of his assorted businesses. I started out in law school, hated it, quit, and went to work as a mechanic in a downtown garage that only dealt with sports cars—I'd always liked tinkering with engines. I went to see my father, tried to level with him and tell him I wanted to be an engineer. You know, man to man. Well, predictably enough, it didn't work. Looking back, I suspect I was probably the first person who'd ever stood up to him and refused to do what he wanted. He was livid—threatened to cut me out of his will, all the usual stuff. My mother was livid too, at the thought of her only son working in a garage ... whatever would all her friends think? Unfortunately a week later my father had a fatal stroke, for which my mother lost no time in blaming me—all the stress I'd caused him was the reason for his death. I was just young enough and naïve enough to believe her, and it wasn't until a couple of years later that his physician told me that for four or five years my father had been a prime candidate for a stroke and had refused to change his life style one iota.'

'That's a terrible story, Stephen.' Joanna rested her hand on his arm. 'I'm so sorry.'

He looked down at the slender fingers resting on his sleeve, with his forefinger tracing the delicate blue veins under the smooth skin. Then he raised his head, grey eyes meeting green, and between them leaped a spark of sexual awareness that each now knew could sweep them into an all-engulfing passion. Very gently Stephen replaced her hand in her lap. 'We'd better not start that again,' he said, 'or I won't be responsible for the consequences. Why don't I put on some music?'

He got to his feet, crossing the room to a long set of teak shelving that housed an impressive array of stereophonic equipment, records, and tapes. The plaintive strains of Fauré's *Pavane* drifted into the room. Joanna had got up to put more wood on the fire; as she straightened, watching the orange sparks shoot up the chimney, Stephen came up behind her. He slid his hands around the curve of her ribs to lie flat on her waist, pulling her back against his body and holding her there. She leaned her head on his shoulder, achingly aware of his strength, of the slow seep of his body heat through her clothing, of the lean, hard length of his body. For a moment the contact alone was enough; she closed her eyes to savour it, wishing time would stop and leave her in this blissful state for ever.

A log shifted in the hearth, sending up a shower of sparks. His hands loosened their hold and their bodies separated; the magic moment was over. Joanna bent to pick up her drink, saying with an assumption of casualness that deceived neither of them, 'Is your mother still alive?'

'Yes . . . she remarried a year after my father's death, a widower as wealthy as my father had been, and moved to California with him. She's been there ever since. Every Christmas we send each other an expensive card, but there's very little contact apart from that. She lives her life and I mine.'

Joanna perched on the edge of the hearth. 'And what do you do now? You mentioned a job you wanted to finish.'

'I started off in engineering, discovered that I loved physics and went on to get my Ph.D. I worked for some years in the field of nuclear physics until I became disillusioned with it—the job is a book I'm writing on the subject. And I'm to be a part-time lecturer at the university here, which I think I'll enjoy—a real change. So there you have it.'

Some of it, she thought inwardly. The setting, the background, and one of the characters: the lonely, dark-haired young man treading his solitary course. But what of the rest? What of the beautiful Laura? What of the child of that marriage?

He was gazing into the flames again, the firelight delineating the strongly carved lines of his face and his deepset, shadowed eyes. For the first time it occurred to her to wonder whether she wanted to hear the rest of the story. He had loved Laura, she was certain of that; what she was afraid of was that he still did ... and she knew she did not want to hear that. She said casually, 'I should give John a call to let him know where I am—I only went out for a walk, you see. I don't want him to think I got lost.'

'There's a telephone in the hall. You know the way?'

She nodded and left the room. When she dialled John's number it rang only once before he picked up the receiver. 'Hello?'

'It's Jo. Just wanted you to know I dropped in to see Stephen——'

'Jo! I was wondering where you were. You couldn't come home, could you, Sis? Léon phoned. He needs some help with a cow that's calving, but I don't want to leave the boys alone.'

Strangely she was conscious of a feeling of relief. 'Of course I can.'

'Bring Stephen with you, why don't you?'

Avoiding this, she answered, 'I'll be home in a few minutes. 'Bye.' Crossing the hall to the living room, she said quickly, 'Stephen, I have to go—John has to go out and there's no one to stay with the boys.'

'I'll run you over.'

'No need—I can go through the woods.'

'I don't like you wandering around alone after dark.'

Warmed that he should concern himself with her safety, she nevertheless retorted, 'This is the country, not the city!'

Stephen had taken his car keys from his pocket. 'What an argumentative creature you are—come along.'

In a few minutes he had pulled up in John's driveway. She said awkwardly, for somehow he had become a stranger again rather than the man who had kissed her and held her so intimately only a short while ago, 'Will you come in?'

'No ... but I do want to see you again, Jo. Tomorrow evening?'

She could no more have refused him than she could have stopped breathing. 'I could come once the boys are ready for bed.'

'I'll see you then.' His manner was almost brusque.

'You do *want* to see me, don't you? You're not just being polite?'

Fractionally his face softened. 'The way I'm feeling right now has very little to do with politeness. Yes, I want to see you. Now off you go.'

Joanna found herself out of the car watching it drive away. Then John joined her, Léon's predicament obviously more on his mind than her meeting with Stephen. 'Don't wait up for me, it might be late. Thanks, Sis.'

In an almost trance-like state she let herself into the house and went upstairs to get ready for bed. The boys were both fast asleep; her bedside clock said quarter past eleven. She undressed slowly, folding her clothes and putting them on the chair. Then, still moving as if she were in a dream, she walked over to the mirror and looked at herself. The lines of her body flowed into one another: the pink-tipped breasts to the concavity of her waist, the swell of hips to the slender length of leg. What would Stephen think if he could see her now? Would he find her desirable?

She shivered, remembering how he had held her, how he had kissed her as though he had been starving and she was the life-giving nourishment he craved. Remembering too how helpless she had been to resist him. Yet a few minutes ago he had not even kissed her goodnight.

Abruptly she turned away from her own image, pulling her nightdress over her head and getting into bed. Tomorrow she would change the sheets and scrub the kitchen floor and give the upstairs a good cleaning. Tomorrow she would see Stephen again ... she would wear something more feminine than the slacks or jeans which were all he ever seemed to see her in, she thought muzzily. A dress maybe, or a skirt. It would be fun to get dressed up. . . .

But when she saw Stephen it did not quite work out that way. The next morning the sheets were billowing on the line like sails in the wind and half a dozen loaves of bread were rising on top of the stove when a tap came at the back door. Joanna called, 'Come in!' not stopping what she was doing. Scrub bucket to her right, she was on her knees on the floor, wielding the steel wool with enough energy that her cheeks were pink.

'Do you ever sit down and do nothing?'

She had been expecting it to be Léon or Della. Pushing back a wisp of hair, she stammered, 'Oh— Stephen. Hello.' She scrambled to her feet. Once again he had caught her at a disadvantage, for her shorts were frayed cut-offs from an old pair of jeans and her shirt a discarded one of John's, several sizes too big for her. He, of course, looked devastating in jodhpurs, high leather boots and a polo shirt.

Her thoughts must have showed in her face, for he began to laugh, and his laughter was so infectious that she found herself joining in. 'Darn you, anyway,' she sputtered. 'I was planning to look very glamorous when I saw you next. And look at me!'

'And I was planning to invite myself for a coffee.' He looked over at the coffee percolator, separated from him and Joanna by a wide stretch of wet floor. 'Another time. But wear something glamorous tonight, Jo—maybe we'll go into town and have a drink.'

'Okay!' In a rush of happiness as spontaneous as it was unexpected, she gave him a wide, generous smile. 'That would be fun.'

Stephen gave her a mock salute with his riding cap. 'See you later.'

She found herself singing about her chores for the

rest of the day. Immediately after supper John chased her out of the kitchen. 'Go and get ready. You've done the work of ten women today, you deserve a night out.'

'Tonight, don't *you* wait up for *me*,' she said.

'So that's the way the wind's blowing, is it?'

She blushed. 'No! Well, maybe . . . I don't know.'

When she came downstairs an hour later, John gave a loud wolf whistle, much to the boys' delight. 'He hasn't got a hope, Sis—very nice!'

She was wearing a flowered peasant skirt with a black velvet cummerbund and a low-cut frilly white blouse, an outfit that always made her feel deliciously feminine. 'Do I really look all right?' she asked anxiously, quite unaware that that was a question she would normally never have asked.

If John noticed her lapse, he was tactful enough not to mention it. 'Fantastic,' he said firmly. 'Have a good time.'

Joanna threw her mohair coat over her shoulders and ran out to the car. When she pulled up by the rose garden at Stephen's, he must have been watching for her, for he came out of the front door immediately. She got out of her car and walked towards him, her high heels tapping on the pavement. He was wearing light grey slacks and a tweed jacket with an ascot at the neck of his silk shirt; he looked confident and relaxed, with a distinction that came as much from his bearing as his looks. Joanna herself was as tautly wound as a bowstring, her green eyes brilliant, her cheeks flushed. His appraisal of her was lightning-swift; all he said was, 'Hello, Joanna.'

'Hello,' she answered lamely, some of the light dying from her eyes. As he held open the door of the Mercedes for her, she wondered what she had expected: to be swept into his arms and kissed until she couldn't breathe? He showed no signs of wanting to kiss her at all.

As they drove into town they talked of commonplace

things, of Star and Rajah, of Joanna's job and the course
Stephen would be teaching next year. He was a good
conversationalist, well-informed yet with a caustic wit,
and ordinarily Joanna would have thoroughly enjoyed
herself. Yet somehow tonight she found herself on edge;
she would have felt more at ease, more herself, dressed in
her blue jeans and sitting on the floor in front of the fire.
They parked the car in a side street and walked to the
centre of town, did a little desultory window-shopping,
discovering that they had similar tastes in a number of
things, and then went into a cocktail lounge. As she
finished her Piña Colada, Joanna managed to insert a
reference to Stephen's wife in the conversation, rather
smoothly she thought; just as smoothly he passed over it,
refusing to be drawn, and for Joanna the message was
plain: this was to be a pleasant, casual date, where nothing
too personal or overly real was to be discussed. She
refused a second drink on the pretext of having to work
the next morning, and with no apparent regret Stephen
said, 'Perhaps we should head home, then. Or do you
want to stay in town at your apartment as you're on the
early shift?'

It was the logical thing for her to do. Swallowing a
curious disappointment that there would be no tête-à-
tête in front of the fire, Joanna replied, 'It would be
more sensible, I suppose. Although I'd have to give
John a call so he wouldn't be worried.' Then she
exclaimed, 'Of course I can't! My car is at your place.'

'I'll drive in tomorrow after you finish work and get
you.'

'I can't expect you to do that, Stephen.'

'I'd rather that than have you get up so early in the
morning—you work too hard, Jo.'

Perplexed, she looked up at him. Why should he care
how hard she worked? 'Tell you what—why don't you
come to my apartment and have a coffee, and then we'll
decide. It's only a couple of blocks from where you
parked your car.'

And so it was agreed. They strolled along the tree-lined streets to the brick apartment building, and Joanna unlocked her door. 'I haven't been here very much lately,' she apologised. 'It's probably covered in dust.'

In fact it was rather surprisingly neat, its inexpensive furnishings arranged to best effect and enlivened by brightly coloured cushions and attractive indoor plants. Perhaps because she was on her own territory, for the first time that evening Joanna began to relax. The two of them were squeezed into the diminutive kitchen preparing the coffee, Stephen smiling at the collection of cartoons decorating the refrigerator door, when the telephone rang in her bedroom. She frowned. 'Excuse me a sec.'

When she came back into the kitchen a minute later, her face was set. 'I'm sorry, Stephen, I have to go. That was the hospital. They'd called me at home and John had told them I was in town, so on chance they tried here. There's been a five-car pile-up on the TransCanada highway—they need all the extra staff they can get.'

Watching her face, he said calmly, 'Go and change. I'll drive you over.'

'Would you? Thanks.'

In her room she stripped off her finery and pulled on a clean uniform and her flat shoes. In silence Stephen drove her the short distance to the hospital. There were two ambulances at the emergency entrance and the wail of an approaching siren. He said flatly, 'Give me your key—I'll wait at the apartment. You can phone me when you're ready to come home, and I'll come and get you.'

One look at his face and the argument she had been about to make died on her tongue. 'All right. Maybe you could give John a call and tell him what's up.'

He leaned over and kissed her cheek. 'Sure . . . chin up.'

So he had divined her inner fears; she should have known he would. 'See you later.' She got out of the car and disappeared into the building.

CHAPTER SEVEN

IT was four hours before the telephone rang in the apartment. Stephen drove to the hospital and Joanna got into the car, giving him a quick, meaningless smile. 'You must be tired,' she said.

'I slept for a while.'

She leaned back in the seat, closing her eyes so she wouldn't have to talk to him. At the apartment as he unlocked the door, she held out her hand for the key, not looking at him. 'I'm sorry I kept you up so late, Stephen—you'll drive carefully, won't you?'

He pushed the door further open with his foot, his big body herding her in ahead of him. She resisted as best she could. 'I'm tired,' she said, over-loudly. 'Please go now, Stephen.'

'Not until you tell me what's wrong.'

'I've just told you—I'm tired!' To her horror she heard her voice break.

He had closed the door behind him, clicking the latch in place. 'It's more than that—why don't you tell me?' he persisted gently, putting his arms around her rigidly held body and drawing her close. 'What went wrong?'

She was trembling very lightly, like a leaf shaken in the wind; her head was downbent, her fists clenched at her sides. She had not minded him seeing her laughter, her anger, her love for her family; but this was her worst weakness, one that she despised but was seemingly helpless to change. She shook her head blindly. 'All I need is some sleep.'

'Did someone die?'

He had touched a raw nerve. She choked back a sob, but there was another crowding her throat and another, and suddenly she was crying in earnest, her face buried in his shirtfront, her hands blindly clutching at his jacket. He held her, his hands rhythmically stroking her back, until gradually her weeping lessened its intensity. Then he murmured, 'Tell me about it, Jo. You can trust me, I won't tell anyone else.'

In her very bones she knew she could trust him, that he was solid and strong, as dependable as the tides that washed the shore. 'Two people did die,' she quavered. 'In spite of everything that was done for them. But it's more than that—it's me. I just hate that part of my work—accident victims, the blood and pain and shock. I'm a member of the medical team, I'm supposed to be detached and unemotional, and just do my job. I—I do the job. But I can't be detached, it's impossible! And so I end up like this.' She sniffed. 'I need to blow my nose.'

Stephen reached over on the coffee table and grabbed a handful of tissues from the box there. 'Here, blow.' She did so, wiping her reddened eyes, her breath still hiccuping in her throat. Then he said, 'Have you ever made a mistake, done anything wrong, when you've been working with accident victims?'

'N—no.'

'So in other words you're functioning as efficiently as you should.'

She nodded. 'But——'

'But nothing. I would suspect, Jo, if you were to ask, you'd find a fair number of the members of your team have some of the same feelings that you have. Perhaps they're older and more experienced, so they've learned to hide them better, or to control them. Your doctor friend—he must hate it when he loses a patient.'

'Yes, he does. But he doesn't go home and cry his eyes out.'

'We all deal with things in our different ways, Joanna. Maybe he goes home and throws plates at the wall.'

She gave a watery grin at the thought of the methodical Drew doing such a thing. 'But I feel such a coward, Stephen,' she muttered. 'Outwardly I'm calm and collected, but inside I'm a bundle of nerves.'

'That's the truest kind of courage there is, to do what has to be done even though you are a mass of nerves.'

'Oh,' she said doubtfully, for this was a new light on her behaviour.

'It's only those without imagination or sensitivity who can be unmoved by the tragedies of others, Jo.'

She digested this in silence, finally saying, 'So you don't despise me for the way I feel, or for collapsing like this afterwards?'

Stephen gave her a little shake as if to emphasise his words. 'Of course not! I think all the more of you.'

One final confession. 'I've never told anyone about it before.'

'I didn't think you had. I'm glad you shared it with me.'

'I am, too.' She smothered a vast yawn. He was still holding her and it seemed the most natural thing in the world to lean against him and close her eyes. 'I've got to be back at work at seven.'

'Then you'd better get some sleep.'

'Mmm. . . .' She suddenly raised her head, looking straight into his eyes and surprising in them a look of unguarded tenderness that made her heart lurch in her breast. 'Thank you, Stephen,' she said simply, knowing she had no need to explain any further. Sensing that he was going to kiss her, she welcomed it, for it seemed such a natural extension of their closeness. She closed her eyes, letting her hands slide up his chest to hold him; the heat of his skin seemed to burn through his shirt.

Before she had left the hospital she had had a quick shower and changed her uniform, more in an effort to relax her over-strained nerves than in any urge for cleanliness; now as she felt his lips slide down her cheekbone to find her mouth, she was glad that she had, glad that her skin was fresh and clean. The first tentative touch of his lips filled her with a wild sweet joy. Then they were strained against each other with an almost desperate urgency, mouths drinking deep, bodies locked together.

Her fingers were buried in the soft, silky hair at the nape of his neck; she could feel his palms flat against her back, crushing her breasts to his chest. His mouth left hers to explore the hollows of her face, the blue-shadowed eyelids, the curve of cheek. Then they slid lower to the slender length of her neck and the sweet-scented hollow at the base of her throat.

She must have made some tiny sound of pleasure, because Stephen was kissing her again, fiercely, hungrily, as if he could not have enough of her, and with an equal hunger she felt against her the pulse and throb of his masculinity, and his hands sliding down her spine to press her hips to his. Devoured by an aching need of him, she moaned his name.

His hands had moved up her body, clasping her shoulders, then moving to the zipper at the front of her uniform. From a long way away she felt him open it, then push the edges of white nylon fabric apart. His lips were like fire on her skin, moving across the soft hollows of her shoulders. Then his hand touched her breast and she shuddered with pleasure.

'Look at me, Jo.'

Slowly she opened her eyes, allowing him to read in them all her desire. His fingers stroked her breast to its tip. Her lashes flickered and she gasped involuntarily, 'Stephen . . . oh, Stephen!' Untutored though she was, for nothing in her experience had prepared her for the shattering intensity of her own reactions, she knew she wanted to give him all the pleasure he was giving her; her eyes still trained on his, her cheeks flushed with a mixture of shyness and boldness that had she but known it was irresistible in itself, she began unbuttoning his shirt. Under her fingertips was the hardness of bone, the roughness of hair, the smooth planes of muscle: hers to explore and to savour.

She felt him tense at her touch, saw in his face the same mingling of pleasure and pain that must be in hers. She smiled tremulously, tasting her power over him, knowing his over her was impossible to ignore or resist. He muttered, 'I want you so much, Joanna. It's been so long. . . .'

He broke off, as if suddenly aware of what he had said, and the pain that scored his face was her pain. 'Stephen, what's wrong?'

His hands dropped to his sides. He took one step away from her, looking like a man who had been hit in the stomach. Passing a hand over his face, he muttered, 'God, what am I doing? I shouldn't even be here, let alone—Joanna, I'm sorry.'

Feeling as though the bottom had dropped out of her world, she grasped him by the arm. But the incoherent rush of words that had been hovering on the end of her tongue died stillborn. Instead she heard herself say very clearly, 'Stephen, you have nothing to be sorry for. Anything that you did, I wanted as much as you. . . .'

He was looking at her as if he had never seen her before. She shook his arm, frightened by the blank incomprehension on his face. 'Please, can't you tell me what's wrong?' she pleaded.

With an effort of will whose cost she could only guess, he said more strongly. 'I'm sorry, Joanna. It was nothing to do with you, believe me. A ghost from the past . . . óne I wonder if I'll ever be free of.'

'Your wife.'

'Yes . . . Laura.'

'Tell me about her, Stephen.'

His features constricted. 'I don't know if I can. I've never told anyone about . . . what happened.'

With the strange sensation that she was fighting an unknown foe, one shrouded in shadow yet very real, Joanna took him by the hand and pulled him over to the chesterfield, saying prosaically, 'Come and sit down.' He obeyed, resting his head on his hands. A tiny victory, but a victory nevertheless, Joanna knew. She curled up beside him, her feet tucked under her; she had done up her tunic, wanting nothing to remind him of their lovemaking. Still speaking as calmly as if they were discussing the weather, she asked, 'How did you meet her?'

As he began to speak, she sensed that he was no longer aware of his immediate surroundings: that he was a long way away both in space and time. He said quietly, 'It was quite by chance. I was driving from Toronto back to the atomic research station where I worked. It was late, pitch dark. She'd been going in the opposite direction and she'd had a flat tyre, so she was parked by the side of the road. I stopped and got out, to see if I could help. She was the most beautiful creature I'd ever seen ... jet black hair that shone like silk and eyes that were so blue they were almost turquoise, like the colour of the sea on a summer day.'

Briefly he fell silent, lost in memory. Joanna waited, one part of her wanting to tell him to stop, that she did not want to hear any more, but the other part, the part that saw her through the worst ordeals in the hospital, knowing it all had to be said.

'Her name was Laura Scrivener. We began talking about personal matters almost immediately, as if there was no time to waste; she was divorced, she told me. Her first husband had been much older than she, and insanely jealous; the marriage had been a mistake from the first. I found myself telling her about my parents and my work, things I normally never discussed. By the time I'd finished changing her tyre, we'd agreed to have dinner together the following evening. A month later we were married.'

He lifted his head, staring down at his hands. 'I'd never been so happy before. It was as though my whole life had been leading up to that meeting. We bought a big house in Toronto and I commuted back and forth; she was a city person, she wouldn't have liked living at the research station. It was the first time in my life I was glad I had money, because she was so touchingly grateful for everything: the house, the servants, the clothes she could buy, the travelling we did and the parties we gave. If she had a weakness it was that she always liked a lot of people around. There was nothing she liked better than having a houseful of guests, and giving dinner parties and going to nightclubs. I didn't need other people as long as I had her . . . but it pleased her and I went along with it. I thought my happiness was complete when we discovered she was pregnant.' He frowned slightly. 'It's funny, at first she was miserable—said a child would come between us, that we were happy as we were. I could reassure her on that because I was so sure nothing could ever côme between us, and eventually she became reconciled to it. Our daughter Karen was born a year and a half after we were married.'

For the first time since he had started talking he seemed to remember Joanna's presence. He said slowly, 'It used to frighten me sometimes, Jo, I was so happy. I had Laura and I had Karen, whom I adored from the moment she was born. I was very busy at work in those days, but I always took as much time as I could to be with them, and if it was impossible, I never stopped Laura from going out to parties or staying with her friends or even travelling abroad without me. That was how it ended. . . .'

Joanna had been hanging on every word, in her own mind, perhaps uncharitably, forming her own image of Laura: beautiful, yet demanding, taking Stephen's money and filling his home with people whose company he did not always want, then at other times leaving him alone so she could be with her friends. Keeping her thoughts to herself, for they could be quite wrong, dictated by a jealousy it was impossible to eradicate, she asked gently, 'What happened?'

He paused to marshal his facts. 'Two years after Karen was born, there'd been a very important development at the laboratory, one that necessitated a small group of us staying there for a period of two weeks pretty well incommunicado—it was highly confidential work, you understand. I'd been under a lot of pressure all that winter, but I was hoping this would end it, and Laura and Karen and I would be able to go away together. But Laura didn't want to stay alone while I was gone, so we arranged for her and Karen to go to the Caribbean for two weeks, and I would join them down there. I wasn't too happy about her choice of location, because there'd been a fair bit of political unrest in the area, although of course it was being played down because of the tourists. But she was always headstrong and I decided I was worrying too much. So off they went, and I buried myself at the research station.' His voice was carefully devoid of emotion when he went on. 'At the end of the two weeks I went home to get packed, and found a message for me to call the manager of the hotel where Laura was staying. To make a long story short, she had told him she was going to stay with friends for a few days but he should hold her rooms because she would be back; he wanted to know if my reservation was still in effect. She hadn't left the name of the friends, nor had she come back ... it was like Laura to change her plans, so I wasn't overly concerned. However, when I arrived, there was no message from her, and when I checked with one or two people whom we knew there, they hadn't even seen her.' He finished abruptly, 'I've never seen either of them again. Laura or Karen.'

'Stephen! But what could have happened?'

'I went to the police, of course. Over the previous six months there'd been several very nasty incidents, and it's possible they were abducted and murdered. There was never any trace of their bodies, but that's hardly surprising. There are dozens of little islands down there and, of course, the waters are infested with sharks.'

His brutal honesty horrified her. 'But Stephen, that's terrible!'

His eyes like stones, he looked over at her. 'Oh, yes. But do you know what's even worse? I had lots of time to think after they disappeared, you see. I found myself remembering little things in the marriage that had seemed trivial at the time. Laura's impatience with the demands of my work, her dismay when she first found out she was pregnant, the amount of time she left Karen with her nanny so she could go to parties. The way she flirted sometimes with other women's husbands.' He ran his fingers through his hair. 'I despised myself for even thinking it, but I found myself wondering if for some reason she'd had enough of me, and had simply chosen to disappear.' Ignoring Joanna's shocked exclamation, he went on ruthlessly, 'So I hired a tracing service. But even they didn't turn anything up. There'd been dozens of commercial planes in and out of there since she'd disappeared, as well as private planes, and yachts and boats. It was hopeless. . . .'

'You never found out what happened?'

'No.'

'Stephen, how dreadful! It would almost be better to know they'd been killed, than to be left wondering for the rest of your life. Never knowing. . . .'

'There's one more thing. A year ago—three years after they disappeared—I met someone who'd known Laura when she was still married to her first husband. His story of that marriage was somewhat different from Laura's. If Bill Scrivener was jealous of Laura, he perhaps had cause, according to this man. He was so convincing that I did something I've sometimes regretted since then: I divorced her. Provided you give the courts reasonable proof that you've tried to trace the person, you can do that.'

'And you've never heard a word from her?'

'Never. You see what it's done to me, Jo—either Laura was a tragic victim of violence, in which case all my love and trust in her was real, validated. Or else she was quite another person, a woman who lied and cheated and deceived. And, worst of all, who stole my child from me.'

'You'll never know which she was,' Joanna whispered, appalled.

'That's right. Whicn means I'll never be free of the past. That divorce is a travesty. I'm still married to Laura, I always will be.'

'So that's why you hold yourself so aloof, why you don't want to get involved.'

'It's why I shouldn't be here with you now, Joanna.'

Unconsciously she leaned towards him, her hands outspread in appeal. 'But—but you're attracted to me, aren't you, Stephen?'

His lips had a bitter twist. 'Oh, yes. There's no faking that, is there? You're the only woman who's gotten anywhere near me in the last four years—perhaps because you're so different from Laura. But it can't go anywhere, Jo. I'll never marry again. I made that vow four years ago and I won't change it.'

She wanted to argue with him, but she had no idea what to say. Her head whirling from a combination of exhaustion and too much emotion, she felt ridiculously like crying again. Trying to speak briskly, she said, 'In an hour's time I've got to leave for work. I think I'll go and have a shower to see if it'll help keep me awake and then have some breakfast.' More gently she added, 'You look worn out, Stephen. Why don't you lie down for a while before you head for home?'

'Let me at least cook you some breakfast.'

About to say no, she wondered if the activity wouldn't be what he needed; it might remove that grey, drawn look from his face. 'Bacon and two eggs,' she said pertly. 'There are oranges in the vegetable compartment, and the coffee——'

'—is in the can marked tea.'

She actually laughed out loud. 'How can you even suggest such a thing?'

In one lithe movement Stephen got to his feet. His shirt was still unbuttoned and in a sudden flashback she remembered the feel of the smooth, taut flesh over his ribs. Her eyes dropped. 'I won't be long,' she mumbled, and beat a quick retreat.

As she showered and dried her hair and put on her uniform again, Joanna was conscious of two things: of feeling surprisingly wide awake considering she had not had any sleep at all; and of a growing sensation of cold anger within her, an anger directed at the absent Laura. Somehow she did not think Laura was dead, for Laura did not sound the type to expose herself to any unnecessary danger. No, she was undoubtedly alive and flourishing, having heartlessly abandoned Stephen for bigger game, and for warped motives of her own having decided to leave her whereabouts a mystery. She, Joanna, had no proof of this, not one iota. But she would have been willing to bet a considerable sum of money that she was right.

In the kitchen Stephen had produced a very creditable breakfast. It was a small, narrow room, too small for two people when one of them was as large as he; their knees bumped under the tiny table, their physical proximity only emphasising the constraint that had fallen between them. Joanna could not very well share her suspicions of Laura with him, nor could she find in herself the courage—or was brashness a more appropriate word?—to enquire if he would have asked her to marry him had Laura not been an impediment. As for Stephen, perhaps he was regretting his confidences; largely in silence he ate the meal he had prepared, then got up to clear it away. 'You don't have to do that,' Joanna said awkwardly. 'I'll do it when I get home.'

'The only thing you'll be fit for when you get home is bed. Do you want me to drive you to work?'

'No, the walk'll do me good.' Desperate to break through their trivial conversation to the real person, she said, 'Stephen, please have a sleep before you start home—it's dangerous to drive when you're overtired.'

His face softened. 'I promise. It's nice of you to worry about me.'

'Didn't Laura?'

It was the wrong thing to have said. 'I don't want to talk about her any more, Joanna.'

Feeling very much snubbed, she said stiffly, 'I'm sorry. I guess I'd better go, it won't hurt to be a bit early. Just make sure the door locks when you leave, will you, please?'

He nodded, making no move to touch her or kiss her goodbye, the black-haired Laura between them as literally as if she had been there in the flesh. 'Goodbye.'

No mention of when he would see her again, Joanna thought miserably as she let herself out and began walking down the path; there was a light drizzle falling, which seemed entirely suited to her mood.

Mercifully the hospital was not very busy, and at noon the head technician sent her home to catch up on her sleep. The first thing she saw as she turned into her drive was the black Mercedes still parked by the kerb; so Stephen had not left. Her heart lifted. Slipping the key in the latch, she very quietly opened the door and stepped inside, closing it just as quietly behind her. Leaving her shoes by the door, she padded softly into the living room.

He was asleep on the chesterfield, his long body relaxed, his breathing deep and regular. He looked younger in sleep, more vulnerable; his lashes were dark and very thick. Her breath suddenly caught in her throat as quietly, without fuss or fanfare, she recognised consciously what she must have known subconsciously for some time: she loved him. That was why she resented Laura so bitterly, and why her heart ached for him in his dilemma. And that was why her body had awakened to his touch as though she had been waiting only for him. She loved him. So very simple, so seemingly inevitable, so right.

Lost in the wonder of her discovery, she did not look to the future at all. Her lips curving in a faint smile, she tiptoed to her bedroom, stripped off her uniform and got into bed, her last thoughts of Stephen, sleeping only a few feet away from her . . . Stephen, whom she loved.

CHAPTER EIGHT

JOANNA awoke from a confused dream in which the boys were clamouring for their supper yet the refrigerator was found to be completely empty. Rubbing her eyes to dispel the vision of bare, chrome-plated shelves, she stared at the clock. Five-fifteen. What on earth was she doing at the apartment? John would be worried sick about her. Jumping out of bed, she hurried into the living room to the telephone.

Stephen was sitting in the armchair reading. In a rush of memory the past twenty-four hours flooded back into her consciousness. 'Oh! I—I'd forgotten. . . .' She began to back towards her room, horribly conscious of her lack of attire, for she had been sleeping in only her bra and panties.

He stood up, the book falling unnoticed to the floor, and something in his eyes made her halt her retreat. As he began walking towards her, she made one last valiant effort. 'I must phone John—he'll be worried,' she stumbled.

'I phoned him earlier and explained that you were sleeping. I'll drive you home after we've had dinner.'

His voice was matter-of-fact. Why then was her heart racing in her breast? He had reached her now ... mesmerised, she felt his hands clasp her shoulders and draw her close to him. Then they left her shoulders to slide down her back to her waist. Tantalisingly slowly they stroked the flatness of her belly and then, as she had known they must, they reached her breasts, cupping the fullness of her flesh.

She swayed towards him, unconsciously raising her face for his kiss. But instead of kissing her, he swung her up into his arms, carrying her through the half open

115

door into her bedroom. Then she was on her back on the tumbled sheets and he was covering her body with his own, supporting his weight on his elbows as he bent to kiss her. She was more than ready for him. Her lips parted; her eyes were slumbrous with desire. She began to remove his shirt, her slow, deliberate movements a provocation in themselves.

It was a kiss that seemed to last for ever. Lips brushed and clung, from gentle to fierce and back again until Joanna thought she would faint with the pleasure of it. Finally Stephen raised his head, his eyes intent on her face as first he shrugged off his shirt and then undid the belt of his trousers and pushed them down over his hips. A delicate flush suffused her cheeks. He rolled over on his back, pulling her to lie on top of him, the feel of his body under hers burning itself into her brain. When he undid her bra and it followed the rest of their clothes to lie on the floor, she quivered with delight to feel the softness of her breast against the tangled hair on his chest. He ordered softly, 'Look at my hands, Joanna—watch what they're doing.' His long lean fingers were rhythmically stroking her breast, caressing the nipple; she did not think she had ever seen anything so beautiful, and her whole body sang with the joy of it and ached for fulfilment.

The only sound in the room was the mingling of their breathing, fast and shallow. His hands had left her breasts and were everywhere, smoothing her skin, searching for places that made her arch and tremble in response, eliciting in her a storm of emotion that it was impossible to deny. Stephen had flung her on her back, hovering over her, protection and assault at the same time, all tenderness and fierce demand. His lips had found her breast; she pressed his dark head to her body, her hips writhing under his in an instinctive demand of their own.

She had never known it could be like this ... oh God, how she wanted him! Digging her nails into his back, she pulled him closer with all her strength, wanting to give to him as he was giving so bounteously to her. Then she felt his hand slide down her body to touch her where no one had ever touched her before; she cried out his name as wave after wave of sensation broke over her, drowning her, until there was only the sound of her own voice crying over and over again, 'I love you . . . I love you. . . .'

She felt the shock run through his body. Felt him rear up, so that cool air struck her skin. Dazed, she opened her eyes, searching his face. Naked desire, clearly to be read . . . but more than that, pain, bitterness, confusion. Jolted back to reality, she touched his cheek with her fingers. 'Stephen, what's wrong?'

The words were wrenched from him. 'You mustn't say that, Jo.'

'Say what? That I love you? But——'

'You mustn't say it!' he repeated more strongly. 'It's all wrong, Joanna, because I can't love you back. She'll always be there, between us—don't you see that?'

Intuitively she did the only thing possible, sensing that his pain and frustration were every bit as agonising as hers. Turning on her side, she put her arms around him almost as if he were one of the boys, or John. 'It's all right,' she said softly. 'I do see. Just lie still.'

His head fell on her shoulder. He was shuddering, as if he had been struck by a whip. She held him close, gently kneading the muscles at the nape of his neck, beginning to understand something of the bonds that held John and Sally together. There was sexual passion, certainly, a primitive drive in the blood as necessary as the air one breathed. But there was also the tenderness that filled her now, the need to comfort and to understand; and underlying all this new knowledge, to be shared with no one, was a slow, burning anger against Laura, who had crippled a man worth ten of her, leaving him neither husband nor widower, married nor free.

For a long time Stephen lay very still in her arms, until she wondered if he had fallen asleep. Then he moved very slightly. 'I think you do understand, don't you, Jo? I can only thank you—you're far more generous than I deserve.'

'You deserve the very best, Stephen. Better than I.'

'Don't say that. You're a beautiful woman, Joanna, beautiful in body and soul.'

She felt tears crowd her eyes and spill over, trickling down her cheeks to fall on his skin. He freed himself from her arms, wiping her face with an edge of the sheet. 'Don't cry—I don't want to make you unhappy. You're so different from Laura, Jo. I keep saying that, don't I? But if anyone can free me from the past, it will be you, I know it. And I know something else—I want to keep on seeing you. I have to. Are you willing to do that?'

Unable to speak, she could only nod, her eyes brilliant with unshed tears. It was the first sign of hope he had given her; it could only confirm in her the sure knowledge that he was the one man she needed.

He leaned across and kissed her, a kiss without passion; it was rather a pledge, an unspoken commitment, and she accepted it as such. With an attempt at normality, he said, 'We'd better get up. I'll take you out for dinner and then we'll head home. Can I come over and visit you at John's tomorrow evening?'

She smiled at him, all her love for him unabashedly shining in her face. 'Of course you may.'

As they dressed, went out for dinner, and drove back to the farm, there was between them an unspoken intimacy, a kind of easy companionship that was something new in their relationship, forged perhaps in the passion and closeness they had shared. Joanna was almost afraid to trust in it. But as the June days passed, spring merging into summer, it not only remained with them, it deepened and intensified. They rode together on the dunes; they walked in the orchard; occasionally they met in town for a movie or a theatre date; they spent evenings at the farm. And Joanna came slowly to believe in the astonishing and miraculous fact that Stephen wanted to be with her and enjoyed her company. She sang at her work, whether at the hospital or the farm, and the soft new radiance in her face made John smile to himself. She made no secret of her happiness, so that inevitably it spilled over on Stephen: he laughed more often, and his eyes lost that haunted, bitter look. Somehow, by a kind of mutual consent, they did not allow the passion between them to flare into the open again. They both knew it was there, for it needed only the touch of a hand, a goodnight kiss, sometimes even a glance, to kindle it to life. But for the moment they were content to leave it in abeyance; instinctively Joanna knew that when the time was right then the fulfilment they both wanted would follow as naturally as day follows night.

As it happened the circumstances were to be far different from any she could have imagined. It was only five days until Sally was due home. Joanna had arranged to take her holidays to coincide with Sally's arrival, knowing her presence would smooth the domestic routine; she had also saved a couple of extra days to be home beforehand and do some much-needed spring-cleaning. It had been decided to turn the back parlour into a temporary bedroom for Sally and John, as it was downstairs, so Joanna had washed the walls and the curtains and cleaned the windows, and was applying a coat of wax to the hardwood floor when the telephone rang in the hall. Hastily she rubbed her hands on the cloth and went to answer it. 'Hello?'

'Joanna? It's Stephen.'

An undefinable note in his voice made her say sharply, 'Is something wrong?'

He sounded very far away. 'Could you come over?'

'Now, you mean?'

'Yes . . . I—I'll see you in a few minutes.' The receiver clicked down and the connection was cut.

For a moment Joanna stared at the instrument in bewilderment, as if it could answer the questions whirling in her brain. Then she raced upstairs, pulling off her work clothes and grabbing a pair of slacks and a crocheted sweater. Downstairs again she wrote a quick note for John and then got in her car. It seemed important to hurry. As she reversed, gravel shot from under her wheels; and then she was bouncing down the driveway, rutted from yesterday's heavy rains.

The lilac was in full bloom at Stephen's, the tall bushes covered with great masses of fragrant purple and white blossoms. At any other time Joanna would have stopped to admire them. Today she parked by the house and ran up to the front door. It was unlocked. She walked in, the silence of the big house an almost tangible presence. It was a house that needed a wife and children, she found herself thinking. If only she could be that woman. . . . 'Stephen?'

No answer— She went through the entrance hall into the living room. Empty, its elegant simplicity a mockery to her growing fear. Back into the hallway, a quick look in the kitchen, also empty, and then through to the back of the house, and the library. Stephen was there, standing in the middle of the room, his back to her. For a moment all other considerations fled in the face of pure relief. 'Stephen?' she said tentatively. Then, more loudly, for he did not seem to have heard her, 'Stephen, I'm here.'

As he turned to face her, she drew in her breath sharply. His face was ashen-pale, his eyes blank with shock; all his movements were unco-ordinated, as if his limbs did not quite belong to him. He was clutching a piece of paper in one hand.

Swiftly she covered the distance between them, grasping him by the elbows, almost afraid that he might fall. 'What's wrong? Tell me——'

He stared down at the vivid little face upturned to his as if he was not quite sure who she was. Or as if he was seeing another, very different, face, she thought sickly. 'Tell me what's wrong,' she repeated, a note of desperation in her voice. His eyes dropped to the crumpled paper in his fist. Without saying a word he held it out to her. She took it and spread it out flat. It was a telegram. At first the words all seemed to run together, blurring in front of her eyes. Then they became separate entities, bearers of a coherent, brutally brief message that only gradually seeped its way into her brain. It was dated the day before, she saw, from a place in the United States, Stony Creek, North Carolina.

Regret inform you of death of wife Laura Marguerite Moore. Please advise at above address arrangements for daughter Karen Elizabeth Moore.

A telephone number followed and a man's name, Jonas Bryson.

She read it again, and a third time. Laura was dead. But dead in an unknown place in the southern States, not in the Caribbean, and dead only recently, not four years ago. And Karen, Stephen's daughter, was alive. She would be six years old now. . . . 'What will you do?' she asked in a level voice.

Her question seemed to break through his self-imposed silence. He said hoarsely, and Joanna did not need to ask of whom he spoke, 'She was alive. All this time she was alive. She took Karen from me and left me, knowing I wouldn't find them . . . how could she have *done* that? How *could* she have?'

There was no answer to his anguished questions. 'Perhaps when you go down there—because you'll go, won't you?—you'll find out,' she answered as calmly as she could.

He drew a deep, ragged breath. 'Yes, I'll have to go.'

'Your daughter is alive, Stephen. That much you know.'

'Yes . . . I haven't seen her since she was two, I don't even know what she looks like.'

'She'll be yours now—she can come here and live with you.'

Her heart ached for him as he looked around the pleasant, sunlit room, obviously trying to orient himself. 'I'd better phone this Jonas Bryson, I guess. Joanna, will you come with me?'

'To North Carolina? To get Karen?' He nodded. 'I'd have to get back before Sally gets home, that's the only thing.'

'We'd go tomorrow.'

She blinked. 'Yes, I could go.'

Briefly he squeezed her shoulder, a faint smile touching his mouth. 'Good girl! I'll go and phone. Be back in a minute.'

It was nearer fifteen minutes before he came back in the room. Joanna was standing by the glass doors looking out over the garden, where the trees were now decorated in nature's full palette of greens; she was remembering another time, a moonlit night when she had walked in the woods to the calling of an owl, and Stephen had kissed her . . . what difference would it make, this new knowledge that Laura was dead? That she had wilfully deceived him and cheated him of four years of his daughter's life? Would it finally free him from the past, free him to love again? His voice broke into her reverie. 'I've spoken to Mr Bryson, and we can pick Karen up at any time. I was lucky enough to get reservations tomorrow, flying through Boston to Charlotte, coming back two days later. And I've made arrangements to rent a car at the Charlotte Airport.'

'Well, you do move fast!'

'You haven't changed your mind?'

'No, I'll come with you. I'd better go home, I must finish the cleaning and get packed.'

'Take summer clothes, it'll be warm down there. I'll

pick you up at seven—we have to get the first flight to Halifax to make our connection to Boston.'

Feeling rather as though she had been picked up by a whirlwind and tossed around until she was disorientated, Joanna said faintly, 'I'll see you tomorrow then—'bye.'

Stephen's answering goodbye was preoccupied; he made no attempt to kiss her or to accompany her out to her car. It was ridiculous to feel hurt by such a small thing, she lectured herself firmly as she drove back to John's. But she could not rid herself of a strange, uneasy feeling in the pit of her stomach. Nothing to do with Karen, or at least she didn't think so. It was because of Laura, that shadowy figure who had haunted the relationship between her and Stephen from the beginning. It was crazy, but she was afraid ... afraid that even from the grave Laura would somehow come between them. Stephen had never told Joanna that he loved her, nor had she ever repeated those magic words since the day in her apartment; despite that, the intimacy between them had fostered in her a quiet confidence that their future lay together. Surely this startling new development could only be for the best?

Joanna had done very little travelling in her life, and consequently she was entranced by her window seat on the jet that flew them to Boston, and by the breakfast brought to her on a plastic tray by the highly decorative stewardess. They had a two-hour wait in Boston. At Joanna's insistence they spent most of the time sitting on a bench outside the international terminal watching the constant coming and going of travellers, people relaxed, harassed, worried, bored. Strange accents and foreign languages regaled her ears, punctuated at regular intervals by the screaming of jets taking off for destinations all over the world. Then they were in their own plane, racing along the runway and boring up through the clouds into the clear blue sky above. Unfortunately once one could no longer see the ground the novelty rather wore off flying, Joanna soon discovered; Stephen had been in an uncommunicative mood all day, something in his face forbidding her from asking too many questions; she read the flight magazine and the safety card, ate yet another meal, and fell asleep.

A change in the sound of the engines awoke her as they began the descent into Charlotte. She touched up her lipstick and brushed her hair, smoothing the skirt of her beige linen suit. Back down through the clouds until she could see trees and fields and ribbon-like grey highways, then the neatly laid out streets of a city. As always the runway seemed to rush up to meet them. The tyres bumped once, twice, and the flaps screamed in the wind. Then they were taxiing up to the gate.

It was not until after she and Stephen had collected their luggage and he had signed the documents for the car that they went outside. The heat hit Joanna like a blow, a still, humid heat under a glaringly blue sky. Their car had been parked in the sun. Its interior was like an oven, so that Joanna wilted visibly. 'Once we get going the air-conditioning will cool it off,' Stephen remarked. 'All set?'

He was right. As they drove through the city to the interstate highway the air-conditioner sent a steady stream of cool air into the car and gradually Joanna began to relax, slipping her feet out of her high-heeled shoes and taking off her jacket. Wide-eyed, she began to look around her. The highway was four lanes wide, edged with grassy banks and tall, luxuriant trees, far taller than their more northern relatives. The gas station signs were unfamiliar, the speed limits in miles per hour. 'I can't believe we've travelled so far in such a short time,' she murmured. 'Oh, look at that gorgeous tree with the pink blossoms, Stephen—I wonder what it is.'

'I have no idea. Get out the map, would you, Jo? I think we turn left beyond Statesville, don't we?'

'On to Route 40.'

The car ate up the miles, for the roads were well kept and very straight, if a trifle monotonous. It was not until they were in the mountains that Stephen checked the map and found his way to the Blue Ridge Parkway. 'I made reservations at a country inn near Stony Creek,' he said. 'I thought we would be better off going to see Karen first thing in the morning rather than late at night when we were tired.'

It was his first mention all day of the purpose of their trip. 'That was wise,' she said casually. 'Does she know we're coming?'

'I asked Mr Bryson to tell her,' His brow furrowed. 'You know, there was something a touch off key in my conversation with him, but I'm damned if I can put my finger on it. I hope it's nothing important. . . .'

'It will probably be difficult for you and for Karen at first,' she ventured. 'She may not even remember you.'

'Do you think I haven't thought of that?' he replied grimly. 'Look at the mountains over on your left, Jo—aren't they lovely?'

Subject of Karen closed, she thought wryly, certain that his few, terse words concealed a deep anxiety about his little daughter, a child he might not even recognise should he pass her in the street. Certainly she would not recognise him. She sighed, turning her attention to their surroundings.

From a tourist brochure in the dash of the car she discovered that the parkway extended over four hundred miles from the Shenandoah Park in Virginia to the Great Smoky Mountains of Tennessee, always curving along the crest of the Appalachians. On either side of the road the rounded, tree-covered peaks vanished into the haze. Grass edged the road and the bright colours of wildflowers: fire-pink and butterfly-weed, purple spiderwort and beard-tongue. The shiny massed leaves of rosebay rhododendrons darkened the woods, for it was too early for them to be in flower, but

as the car climbed steadily higher, they saw banks of
purple rhododendrons and pale mountain laurel, and
the spectacular orange blooms of flame azalea waving
in the breeze.

It was a road designed for a far slower pace than the
interstate they had left only a short while before, for it
had numerous look-offs over the valleys and hills, and
its total lack of commercial development was in itself
restful. The bridges had been built with natural stone,
while the tunnels were hewn from the living rock,
overhung with giant oak and magnolia trees. They saw
fields with cattle and sheep; caught a quick glimpse of a
white-tailed doe and two fawns disappearing into the
forest; watched the sun sink behind the mountains in a
blaze of colour that rivalled the azaleas. Finally Stephen
spoke. 'I think we turn off just ahead. Watch out for
signs for the Smoky Mountain Inn, will you?'

Fortunately they had no trouble finding it, for
Joanna, at least, was getting very tired. It was reached
by a narrow lane that climbed up the mountainside, the
gardens even at dusk a mass of colour, the view a
magnificent outlook of the valley and the purple hills.
Stephen checked in, then drove the car to the end of the
far wing of the inn. There was a verandah with rocking
chairs, inviting one to sit and admire the view; the air
was filled with the scent of roses. 'We have adjoining
rooms,' he said briefly. 'The dining room closes in half
an hour, so maybe we should go and get something to
eat right away.'

Joanna was hungry, even though all they had done
all day was sit; she was also desperately tired,
disorientated by the distances they had covered and the
transition from familiarity to this beautiful but subtly
different land. 'I guess we'd better eat,' she said flatly.

All too briefly he squeezed her shoulder. 'It'll make
you feel better.'

The dining room was like a spacious formal garden
with its white wicker furniture, deep green carpet, and

artfully arranged hanging plants and baskets of flowers; the service was excellent, the waitress's soft, Southern drawl delighting Joanna. She chose a fresh fruit salad accompanied by a glass of sparkling rosé wine, her eye noting all the details of the menu, the décor, and their fellow guests. Stephen was largely uncommunicative, lost in his own thoughts; while Joanna might have wished him in a different mood, she was wise enough to leave him alone. After the meal they walked back to their wing past beds of summer flowers flanking the shadowed shrubbery, the night a velvet blackness studded with stars. Outside her door they stopped. It was very quiet, for most of the other guests seemed to have gone to bed; perhaps, she thought hopefully, he would kiss her goodnight. And so he did, the merest touch of his lips to her cheek. 'Sleep well, Joanna.'

She gazed up at him uncertainly. His eyes were black as the night and just as impenetrable, his expression closed against her. 'I hope you will, too,' she murmured.

Something in her bearing must have touched him. 'I'm not good company, I know, Jo, and I'm sorry—I guess I can't get tomorrow off my mind. But I *am* glad you're here.'

As his rare smile lit up his face, she felt her heart melt with love for him. With more assurance she said simply, 'That's good. Goodnight, Stephen.' She went into her room and closed the door.

It was a delightful room, with flowered wallpaper, a pristine white cover on the double bed, and old-fashioned maple furniture; the bathroom was a miracle of cleanliness and sparkling chrome, nothing old-fashioned about it. She should have been enjoying it all . . . why then did she feel so lonely, as if Stephen had deserted her in an alien place? Don't be silly, she told herself firmly. He's next door, within twenty feet of you.

But he doesn't want your company, the nasty little

voice argued back. He wants to be alone ... to remember Laura.

He's worried about meeting his daughter, that's all! It's nothing to do with Laura.

Well, if that's what you want to think. ...

Joanna unlocked her suitcase far more vigorously than was necessary, shaking out the dress she intended to wear tomorrow and hanging it up in the closet. Purposely she strewed some of her make-up on the dresser and left her shoes by the chair, anything to make the room looked more lived-in. Then she had a long, luxurious bath, squandering the hot water in a way she never would have at home. It relaxed the tension from her muscles and quietened the angry little dialogue in her brain; but it did not make her feel any sleepier. She slipped a long robe over her naked body and regarded herself solemnly in the mirror. She had made the robe herself out of a heavy off-white cotton, edging the wide sleeves and the hem with turquoise braid; a friend at the hospital had embroidered a profusion of vivid flowers and leaves around the plunging, laced neckline.

Wide-awake green eyes met their reflection in the mirror. She could read. She could try and sleep. Or—the green eyes brightened—she could very quietly slip outside and sit on the chair outside her door, and look out over the scattered lights of the valley. There would be no one around at this time of night. That's what she would do.

Creeping outdoors on bare feet and finding herself as alone as she had anticipated, she sat down on the rocking chair, leaned her head back on its high back, and closed her eyes. Somehow out here she did not mind being alone. From the far end of the inn came the faint echo of laughter and the slam of a car door. The lightest of breezes touched her face, not strong enough to disturb the rhododendrons or the spiked leaves of the tall holly bushes that edged the driveway. With one foot she began to rock the chair, finding it mercifully silent, soothed by the gentle, rhythmic movement, back and forth, back and forth. . . .

'Couldn't you sleep?'

Her eyes flew open, and the chair jerked to stillness. 'Stephen! You scared me.'

'Sorry, I didn't mean to frighten you. I went for a walk—there's a path down the slope that leads to a golf course.'

'So you can't sleep either.'

'No.' Only one word, but behind it she sensed a welter of pent-up emotion, and once again she was conscious of a black-haired woman laughing at her from the shadows.

But Laura was dead . . . whereas she, Joanna, was very much alive. She was the one with Stephen now, not Laura. She stood up, casually shaking out the folds of her gown. 'As we both can't sleep, why don't you show me the path?'

He had taken one quick, involuntary step towards her. Now he hesitated, his eyes trained on her face. 'You'd have to put something on your feet—the ground is rough.'

'I'll get my sandals.' Nearly at her door, she suddenly turned to find him right behind her, so close she could feel his breath on her cheek. Whatever she had been going to say fled from her mind.

There was a silence that to her overstretched nerves seemed to last for ever. It was he who broke it, his question very matter-of-fact. 'Is your door locked?'

'No.'

He reached round her and opened it, ushering her in the room ahead of him, closing the door behind him and slipping the lock in place, its metallic click sounding very loud.

She had left the night light on. In its soft glow she could see the pulse throbbing at the base of his throat, while his eyes seemed to bore right through her. Deep within her she knew what was going to happen, here in a hotel room miles from home, and knew it to be right and true, for tonight Stephen needed her as perhaps he had never needed her before. There was only one way she could erase the strain from his face, make him forget the beautiful woman who had robbed him of so much. But it would be more than that, she knew. For tonight, with her body, she could give him all that was hers to give, and from him, surely, receive the fulfilment that she craved. . . .

'Joanna. . . .' His kiss was gentle, almost tentative, so that she held back her own response. He was running his hands up and down her arms, kneading their softness through her robe. 'Maybe I shouldn't be here,' he muttered. 'But, God, I want to be. I need you, Joanna. . . .'

She raised her head proudly, knowing she had to say it. 'I love you, Stephen.'

With something of the same tentativeness, he reached up and stroked the smooth curve of her cheek. 'You said that to me once before . . . I wish I could say it back to you, Jo, but I can't. Something stops me, every time. I may never be able to say it to you.'

Her smile was very grave. 'It's all right . . . I understand.'

'I think you do, don't you?' He stepped back, although he still held her, his hands dropping to find her hands and clasping them strongly. 'Joanna, I want to stay with you tonight.' Briefly his hands tightened their hold. 'But if I do, we both know what will happen, don't we? Because I can't stay with you without making love to you—I want you too much.'

It was her turn to speak. He would not force himself on her, for that was not his way, and were she to send him away, he would go. Neither would he beg from her. The choice was hers. She said, knowing she was taking the irreversible step into womanhood and that nothing would ever be quite the same again, 'I'd like you to

stay, Stephen.' Even as she spoke she was touched by
fear, a simple fear of the unknown, of all the old wives'
tales of pain and disappointment. But mingled with this
was a more complex anxiety: that in her ignorance and
inexperience she would not please him. That he would
find her awkward and shy and afraid, maybe even
ugly. . . .

He must have seen the tremulous flutter of her lashes,
the sudden panic in her eyes. He said quietly, 'Don't be
frightened . . . I'll be very gentle with you, I promise.'
His voice roughened as he drew her into his embrace,
punctuating his words with kisses on her forehead, her
eyes, her cheeks. 'I want you so much.'

As his mouth finally found hers, the last of her fears
fled, for she was wanted and desired by Stephen, whom
she loved more than she had thought it possible to love
a man. His kiss seemed to penetrate to her very soul.
She put her arms around him, exulting in the taut
muscles of his back, the long line of his spine, feeling
him hold her so tightly that she could scarcely breathe.

When he released her, she stood very still, waiting for
what he would do next, trusting in him absolutely. He
said huskily, 'Take off my shirt, Joanna.'

Although there was shyness in the way she blushed,
her hands were steady as she undid the buttons of his
shirt, one by one. He shrugged it off his shoulders,
letting it drop to the floor. 'Now touch me here—and
here.' The feel of her fingers, caressing and exploring
with an entrancing confidence, made him shudder; his
heartbeat pounded against the wall of his chest. His
hands fumbled for the buckle of his belt and then he
was naked.

As he unlaced the front of her gown and pushed it
from her shoulders so that it fell in a crumpled heap on
the floor, her eyes dropped, her hands instinctively
trying to cover herself. He took her wrists, holding
them away from her body. 'You're so lovely, Jo—let me
look at you.' She began to tremble as his eyes wandered

possessively over the pale beauty of her figure, breast, waist, hip and thigh. Then he drew her close to him, and for the first time in her life she felt the lean, hard length of a man's body against her own softness and curves. When he picked her up and carried her to the bed, she only knew she wanted him closer, exulting in his weight and warmth, in his searching hands, his lips that roamed her body. With exquisite care he brought her to the knife-sharp edge of desire, so that she could only welcome his inevitable invasion, unaware of pain or fear. Lost in the vivid storm he had himself called up in her, assaulted by wave after wave of passionate longing, she tumbled into their depths, knowing he was with her, lost as she was in the calm that was the very heart of the storm.

Time had lost all meaning. Slowly Joanna came back to the present, to find their bodies entwined, to feel the strong beat of his heart slowing to normal against her cheek, to see sweat beading his forehead, and in his eyes a tender, quizzical light. 'Oh, Stephen . . . I—I had no idea it was like that. So total. So complete. So——' she sought for the right words. 'So beautiful,' she finished inadequately. 'I don't know how else to describe it. I feel as though I've journeyed a long way.'

He buried his face in her neck. 'And come home—I hope?'

Overwhelmed by a love she could only express in the convulsive tightening of her arms, she hugged him fiercely. 'Truly I have come home.'

He was kissing her neck, nibbling gently at her ear. She lay still in his embrace, suffused with contentment and peace. Gradually her breathing slowed and deepened, and then she slept.

CHAPTER NINE

IT was still dark when she awoke and for a moment she had no idea where she was, tensing against the hold of the man in bed with her. 'It's all right,' Stephen murmured lazily, 'it's me.'

She began to laugh, unable to help herself. 'That's not much good,' she scolded. 'You might at least tell me your name—in case I've forgotten it, you understand.'

He threw his thigh over her legs, drawing her closer. 'You'd better not have forgotten it,' he growled. 'Have you forgotten this as well? And this?'

She gasped with pleasure, feeling a resurgence of the sweet ache of longing for him as his hands stroked the swell of her breasts. Although she had not put it into words, she had sensed that in their first lovemaking he had given more than she, in his concern that she not be hurt; now it was her turn. Made bold by the dark, she began kissing him, delighting in the freedom to touch him wherever she wished and growing ever more confident as she felt him respond. She let her hands wander where they pleased, beginning to learn what pleased him. She gave him tenderness and passion; her innocence and her new-found knowledge; laughter, and at the end as he found release within her, tears of joy.

'Don't cry, sweetheart.'

'It's because I'm so happy.' She reached up and kissed him, her lips soft and warm from their lovemaking. 'Thank you, Stephen.'

He smoothed her hair back from her face, running his fingers through its soft curls. 'It's I who must thank you,' he said very seriously. 'You're so warm-hearted and generous, Joanna. I—I don't want to talk about the past. But I do want to say that I've never been given as

133

much as you have given me tonight.' He hesitated, as though searching for the right words. 'It's a strange thing to say, I suppose, and not particularly romantic, but I feel safe with you. As if you cared for me . . .' His voice was so low she could scarcely hear him. 'I know you wouldn't hurt me, not if you could help it.'

She managed to say with creditable calm, 'Of course I wouldn't hurt you, Stephen,' even while inwardly she was appalled by all the implications of his words. Even when they had made love, had Laura hurt him? Had she only taken from him in their marriage, never giving anything in return? What kind of woman had she been?

His head was lying on her breast, his arm heavy across her body. It would undoubtedly become very uncomfortable, but at the moment she could not have cared less. 'Maybe we should try and get some sleep,' she murmured.

She was sure he was smiling in the dark. 'If you'd stop molesting me, maybe we could.'

Joanna was smiling too as she fell asleep, and was still smiling when she woke up what seemed like only minutes later even though sunlight was streaming in through the curtains. She opened her eyes, rubbing them childishly. Stephen was awake, leaning on one elbow watching her. She yawned and stretched with unconscious provocation. 'Good morning.' Suddenly realising the sheet was down to her waist, she grabbed at it to cover herself.

Stephen was quicker than she. His hand shot out and stayed hers. 'It's a bit late for that, isn't it?' he grinned, his eyes caressing her in a way that brought colour to her cheeks. 'I wish we could stay here, but we can't. Breakfast is in half an hour. I'll go to my own room to shower and I'll come and get you when I'm ready.' She might have thought him too businesslike had he not added, his gaze lingering on the faint blue shadows under her eyes, and the full lips, 'You look like a woman who has been well and truly made love to.'

'So I have been. . . .'

He leaned over and kissed her, and then swung his legs over the side of the bed, reaching for his trousers on the floor. When he left the room a minute later, it felt very empty without him, and suddenly Joanna shivered, hugging her knees to her. The night was over, more beautiful than she could have imagined; but now it was over. It was daytime, the day when they had to go to Laura's house and find Laura's daughter.

Not wanting to think about it, she jumped out of bed and ran to the bathroom, turning on the water full blast. When Stephen tapped on her door half an hour later she was just putting the finishing touches to her make-up. She got up and let him in. He was wearing a pale grey, lightweight business suit, his hand-tailored shirt and silk tie in impeccable taste, gold cufflinks at his wrists; and with the clothes he had donned something else: a remoteness in his manner, a reserve in the cool grey eyes. He had become a stranger, a handsome, immaculately dressed stranger. This could not be the man whose naked body had brought her such delight through the long hours of the night. . . . She said lightly, 'I'm nearly ready.'

It was a relief to turn away from him and go over to the dressing-table, where she carefully applied a frosted coral lipstick and put on tiny gold earrings and a looped gold necklace. Her dress was a slim, very plain sheath, high-necked and long-sleeved, belted in at the waist, its severity denied by the slit on one side that went halfway up her thigh. Her sandals were nothing but a couple of thin leather straps with very high heels. It was an outfit that gave her confidence; she had chosen it with that in mind.

Side by side she and Stephen walked down the long verandah to the dining room. It was already warm with the promise of greater heat to come, and the sum total of their conversation was one or two desultory remarks on the weather. Once in the hotel Stephen said abruptly, 'Do you mind if I get a paper?'

Rhetorical question, she thought wryly. 'Not if I can have part of it.'

So like a long-married couple they sat at the breakfast table reading the newspaper, Joanna already beginning to wish that the day was over. The meal revived her spirits a little: fresh melon, grits, and tiny sausage cakes served with fluffy scrambled eggs and quantities of delicious American coffee. Nevertheless, she was glad when Stephen pushed back his chair. 'Finished?'

'Yes, thanks.' If he could be cool, so could she.

They went outside to the car, where Stephen consulted the map, and her curiosity got the better of her. 'You haven't told me where we're going.'

'To an estate called Belle Maison, a couple of miles west of Stony Creek—about ten miles from here. I have no idea whether it belonged to Laura, or to this Mr Bryson, or to someone else—husband number three, perhaps?' There was an ugly edge to his voice. 'Nor do I have any idea of what we'll find when we get there, apart from Karen, that is. Mr Bryson was singularly uncommunicative when it came to concrete details.' He swung the car out on to the highway.

They missed their turn-off and had to backtrack, so that it took the best part of three-quarters of an hour to reach the entranceway to Belle Maison, two imposing brick pillars with an open wrought iron gate, flanked by thick hedges of holly and rhododendron. The driveway was paved, curving in a semi-circle through a grove of stately pine trees. Then as the house itself came into view Stephen braked, and they examined it in silence.

It was, Joanna decided, a triumph of too little taste and too much money. It was immense. Built of pale yellow brick, its shuttered windows and spacious wings were reminiscent of the Colonial period, while the five huge columns, complete with pedestals and garlanded figures carved in bas-relief, were surely Greek in orgin. Despite the artistically arranged shrubs and trees, it looked horribly new, an excrescence in a landscape that deserved far better.

'Well,' said Stephen. 'Well....' There seemed nothing more to add; however, he shot Joanna a quick conspiratorial glance that heartened her greatly before he drove up to the front door, parked the car, and handed her out with a flourish.

'I should be wearing a crinoline,' she murmured, smoothing her skirt nervously.

'Or a tunic and a laurel wreath.' He pressed the doorbell.

She was not surprised when an elderly butler opened the door, his red jacket bedecked with a great deal of gold braid. Stephen said impassively, 'Mr Moore and Miss Hailey. I am Karen's father.'

Did she imagine the flash of very human curiosity that crossed the butler's austere mask? 'Please come this way, sir, madam.'

They followed him through a vast entrance hall with more pillars, twin curving staircases, and a marble floor on which Joanna's heels clicked alarmingly. Potted palms and avocados stood in the alcoves along with some rather indecent statuary; somewhere a fountain splashed. For all the sunlight that entered through the tall windows, there was something vaguely sinister about Belle Maison, Joanna decided, keeping very close to Stephen; or if sinister was too strong a word, at least something definitely unfriendly. She could not imagine it housing a six-year-old; it seemed designed for the pages of a high-class magazine rather than for ordinary, day-to-day living.

As the butler swung open the set of carved ebony doors that led into the living room, Joanna hung back purposely, wanting Karen to meet Stephen first; this gave her a moment to take in as many details as she could of the living room. It was at least two hundred feet long, with a vaulted ceiling, and three huge bay windows overlooking the back of the estate. A grand piano, marble fireplaces, and suede-covered furniture relieved the starkness of the pure white carpet.

Then something in the quality of the silence dragged her attention back to Stephen. He had stopped dead in front of her. She heard him draw a single, shocked breath. Then she heard a woman's voice say, 'Hello, Stephen.'

Because Joanna loved Stephen, she was attuned to his every mood. In the few seconds that she stood frozen in position behind him, the rigid set of his shoulders and the hands clenched to fists at his sides gave their own message: he had received a severe shock. However, as she deliberately stepped out from behind him, she was subconsciously more or less prepared for what she was going to see, so that her manner was more natural than his. To the black-haired woman so gracefully disposed on the chaise-longue she said coolly, 'Good morning. I would assume you are Laura?'

Across the vivid blue eyes, the most beautiful eyes Joanna had ever seen, there flashed an expression far from beautiful. Then the woman regained control so rapidly that Joanna wondered if she had imagined that momentary slip. 'Yes, I am Laura Moore. And you are . . .?'

This little interchange must have given Stephen the time he needed. He said brusquely, 'Joanna Hailey. We're neighbours.'

'So . . . the girl next door.'

There was nothing Joanna could take exception to in the smile on those exquisitely carmined lips or in the dulcet voice, yet unaccountably she felt herself flush. She said just as sweetly, 'I'm considerably younger than Stephen, of course, but I hardly think I can be called a girl any more.' The unspoken message, considerably younger than you as well, she let hang in the air.

Impatiently Stephen cut in. 'I got a telegram saying you'd died recently. Who the hell sent it?'

Laura gave an indulgent laugh. 'You haven't

changed, have you, darling? You always were one to get right to the point. But, please ... I'm forgetting my manners. Do sit down, both of you, and I'll ring for Bryson to bring some coffee.'

'Bryson?' Stephen said sharply, ignoring her invitation.

'Yes—the butler.'

'I see.' There was a wealth of meaning in Stephen's words. 'Will you stop trying to treat this as a nice little social occasion, Laura, and tell me who sent that telegram? Obviously Bryson didn't.'

'Very well. I did, of course.'

His voice was deadly. 'Perhaps you wouldn't mind explaining why?'

The long black lashes fluttered. 'I didn't know what else to do, Stephen.' With consummate timing the turquoise eyes looked straight at him, blazing with sincerity. 'I desperately needed to see you. But I was afraid if I simply wrote or phoned that you wouldn't come. Hence the ruse of the telegram.'

'With Karen nicely dangled as bait.'

'Karen needs a father, Stephen. I've done the best I can, but it's difficult for a woman on her own. . . .'

Stephen drew another of those short, angry breaths. 'Spare me the martyred mother routine!' He gave their opulent surroundings a caustic look. 'I would rather doubt that you've been on your own, for one thing. Whose house is this?'

The delicately pointed chin was raised bravely. 'It was Richie's house. . . .' She couldn't be faking that quiver in her voice, Joanna thought blankly, walking past Stephen to perch on the arm of one of the deep chairs; neither of the other two even noticed her move.

With heavy patience Stephen demanded, 'And who is Richie?'

'He's dead. He was—my dear friend.'

'In other words he was keeping you. And now that he's dead, you're looking for someone else to do that.'

'Please, Stephen, don't be angry with me——' Laura stood up, the chiffon folds of her smoke-grey lounging robe falling about her feet, her hands held out in appeal.

He took a step towards her, almost as if he was going to seize her and shake her, and then stopped. 'You're telling me not to be angry! Laura, don't you know what you've done to me? For four years I haven't known whether you and Karen were alive or dead. You disappeared without a trace, taking my daughter with you, robbing me of all those years when she was growing up so that now I'm not even sure I'll recognise the child—and you tell me not to be angry!'

'I know. . . .' Her voice broke. 'It was a terrible thing to have done.'

'Terrible—it was criminal!'

'I was desperate, Stephen.' It was she who stepped towards him now, standing very close to him yet not actually touching him. Her make-up was subtle, emphasising rather than disguising her pallor; with a stab of jealousy Joanna saw that the only jewellery she was wearing was a plain gold wedding band. 'If only I could make you understand——'

'Try me.' The grey eyes were hard as steel.

Her face lost in memory, Laura began to walk back and forth in front of Stephen, the grey robe flowing gracefully, her perfume wafting on the air. 'You know about my first marriage, how unhappy it was. Then I met you and it was like the answer to a prayer.' She looked at him, her lips curving, her eyes lingering suggestively on his mouth. 'We were very happy, weren't we?'

Neither agreeing or disagreeing, he said flatly, 'Get to the point, Laura.'

The turquoise eyes searched his face. 'You've changed, darling, you're harder, more difficult to reach. Did I do that? I suppose I must have . . . I have a lot to apologise for. Well, anyway, you'll remember that I was worried about my pregnancy, afraid that a child would come between us and spoil what had been so perfect. And it seemed to me, once she was born, that that was indeed what happened. You changed. You were absorbed in your work, gone so much of the time— although I trusted you, Stephen, don't think for a minute I didn't. But I missed you. And when you were home, it seemed Karen took up so much of your time, time you would once have spent with me.'

'Karen was our daughter, Laura. I loved her, and wanted to be with her. That didn't mean I loved you any the less.'

'I suppose not.' Her head bowed. 'I only know I was unhappy, that things weren't as they used to be. I even used to wonder which you loved more—me or your work. Me or your daughter.'

'*Our* daughter.' His voice was dangerously quiet, and fleetingly Joanna was sure that the other woman was disconcerted.

Laura tossed her head, her hair, fine as black silk, swirling about her slender neck. 'What happened was, I suppose, inevitable,' she said quietly. 'I need love, Stephen, you know that. I was lonely without you——'

'Laura, you're beginning to sound as though I abandoned *you* rather than the reverse. You know I was with you as much as I possibly could be. We'd discussed my work. You knew it was demanding—but just because I was at the research station it didn't mean I'd stopped loving you.'

'I felt as though you had.' There was undoubted dignity in the slim, grey-clad figure.

He muttered an expletive under his breath, going to stand by the fireplace, one arm leaning on the mantel. 'Go on.'

'Karen and I went to the Caribbean for two weeks. The first day I was there, I met Richie. He swept me off my feet, Stephen. You'd gotten so serious. He was fun and lively and had all the time in the world to spend with me. He had to go back to the States a week after I met him, and when he suggested Karen and I accompany him, I agreed. It was only to be temporary, a holiday, a fling—I felt I needed one, and I thought it would do you good to realise that other men found me attractive.'

'I'd have had to have been blind not to have realised that.'

'We went by boat to one of the other islands, and then by private plane here.'

'Covering your tracks.'

With sudden violence Laura said, 'I wanted to frighten you! You'd been taking me for granted—I wanted to change that.'

Stephen's anger flared to meet hers. Grabbing her by the arm, he said roughly, 'You persist in casting me as the villain of the piece—you're rationalising your own actions, and you damned well know it.'

Pliant as grass in the wind, she leaned towards him. Frozen to her chair, Joanna watched, knowing that her presence had been forgotten by the other two, absorbed as they were in their private battle. There was blatant provocation in Laura's next words. 'At least you're looking at me now as though you know I exist.' She slid her hands up his chest, holding on to the lapels of his suit. 'Remember how it used to be, Stephen?' she whispered. 'You haven't forgotten that, have you?'

'I remember,' he said harshly, deep lines scoring his face from cheek to chin. He thrust her away. 'But that was four years ago, Laura.'

'We could be happy again.'

'You mean, now that Richie's no longer around?'

'Don't be crude!'

'What happened?' he taunted viciously. 'Didn't he leave you all this in his will?'

With the first real crack in her composure, Laura muttered, 'No—it goes to his wife.' She attempted a smile, but it was not wholly convincing. 'He felt he was doing the right thing, I'm sure. She's considerably older than I.'

'Hence the telegram—you must have to be out of here fairly soon.'

'You're putting the worst possible interpretation on this, Stephen. Please . . . give me a fair hearing. I know I did a dreadful thing four years ago, and I should have got in touch with you afterwards, but when I saw the island newspapers and knew you were searching for me, I was afraid. . . . But I'm older now, and a little wiser, I hope.' Her voice caught. 'You're not helping me at all, are you? What I'm saying is very simple—I want to come back to you, Stephen.'

Joanna's heart constricted. How could any man resist such an appeal? Let alone Stephen, who had never made any secret of his love for Laura. She found her eyes dragged to him as the silence stretched out. He was staring down at the floor, his fingers clenched on the edge of the mantel so hard that his knuckles stood out, white with strain. He said in such a low voice she could hardly hear him, 'It's too late, Laura.'

'It need not be. I've learned something in the past few months—learned to value what I once had with you, which, for the best of motives, I threw away. I wouldn't throw it away again.'

'Maybe not. But you're forgetting one thing, Laura— I've had four years without you. You're assuming I've made no other attachments in that time.'

Laura's eyes, hard as glass, flickered over at Joanna, sitting so quietly on the chair. 'What do you mean?'

'Maybe I don't want you back.'

'I don't believe that can be true. You can't deny the past, Stephen, or pretend it didn't happen. I'm your wife, the mother of your child.'

'You are certainly the mother of my child, and I want her back, Laura. But you are no longer my wife.'

The perfectly sculpted cheeks paled, and suddenly

Laura looked much older. 'What do you mean? Of course I'm your wife!'

'I divorced you a year ago.'

'You couldn't have!'

'I could and I did. I waited three years, put the appropriate notices in the newspaper, told the judge how I'd tried to trace you when you'd first disappeared and got the divorce.'

'Why?' The word was like a whiplash.

'Quite by chance I met a man called Gerry Stevens—remember him? A friend of your first husband's?' From Laura's face it was obvious she did remember. 'He told me a few things about that marriage that you'd somehow neglected to tell me, and I decided perhaps I'd been a naïve and credulous fool.' His voice was savage. 'I'd trusted you, Laura. I'd believed every word you'd ever told me.'

'Gerry was lying! He hated me—he'd wanted to go away with me, and I wouldn't, and so he always hated me after that.'

'You have an answer for everything, don't you?' Stephen grated. 'What about this, my beautiful ex-wife—do you have an answer for this as well?' He covered the distance between them in two strides, his face taut with a mixture of emotions Joanna could not have begun to decipher. His arms went around Laura, pulling her to him with furious strength. He lowered his head and began to kiss her.

Joanna made a tiny, choked sound of protest. Unable to bear watching them, unable even to be in the same room, she got to her feet, frantically looking around for a way of escape. In the middle set of bay windows was a pair of French doors leading out to a stone-flagged patio. Wrenching the door open, she went outside, not even bothering to see if it closed behind her. The heat pressed down on her like a living, inimical force. Only knowing she had to put as much distance as she could between her and the couple in the living room, she began to run, darting through a gap in the trees.

Underfoot the grass was mowed to a smooth, even green. Briefly she stopped, taking off her high-heeled shoes and carrying them in one hand as she ducked under a couple of pine trees and went through a gap in the holly bushes. Then she slowed down. Ahead of her, surrounded by flowerbeds, was a child's playhouse, charmingly decorated to look like a gingerbread house, its back door opening on a lily pond complete with a miniature bridge and model ships. Sitting on the rocks that edged the pond, listlessly throwing stones into the water, was a little girl.

She looked up when she heard Joanna's approach, and Joanna stopped dead in her tracks. That it was Stephen's daughter she had no doubt, for under the silky, peat-brown hair, which had been elaborately arranged in ringlets, was a pair of level grey eyes. The child said politely, 'Why are you running? It's too hot to run.'

Joanna came closer, subsiding on a white-painted bench at the edge of the pool. 'You're right,' she said feelingly. 'I—I guess I just wanted to get out of the house.'

'I hate the house, too. What's your name?'

'Joanna. Joanna Hailey. And you must be Karen.'

'Did you come here with my father?'

'Yes, I did.'

'My mother told me he was coming. I have to stay out here until she sends for me.'

'Oh.' There seemed no other reply to make to this. For all the child's appearance, for she looked like an overdressed doll in her frilly cotton frock and spotless white shoes and socks, there was intelligence in the piquant little face, and even the possibility of humour. Joanna smiled, all the warmth of her personality clearly visible. 'Your father is anxious to see you, I know,' she said gently.

Karen was busily stirring the water with a stick. 'What's he like?'

Joanna leaned forward, putting all the conviction she could in her words. 'You'll like him, Karen. He's tall and good-looking, and he likes to ride horses and——'

'Do you think he'd teach me to ride? Or is he busy all the time? She added philosophically, 'Richie and my mother were always busy.'

'I'm sure he'd teach you to ride,' Joanna said recklessly. Karen seemed to be assuming she would be living with Stephen—but was that true? What about Laura?

Karen's eyes widened. 'Is that him now?'

Through the trees a man's voice was calling Joanna's name. 'Yes, that's him,' Joanna said equally ungrammatically. Standing up, she called, 'Over here!' Karen stood up too, her eyes very big, and impulsively Joanna took the child's hand in hers. 'It'll be all right, you'll see.'

Stephen came through the same gap in the holly hedge, hesitating momentarily as he saw Joanna and the child standing by the edge of the pool. He was alone. He walked towards them, then dropped on one knee in front of his daughter. 'Hello, Karen,' he said, a note in his voice Joanna had not heard before, his grey eyes very steady.

The little fingers tightened on Joanna's. 'Hello.'

'You probably don't even remember me.' A tongue-tied shake of the head. 'When you first learned to walk, you used to run across the grass to me and grab me by the knees. And then I'd pick you up and swing you way over my head.'

The child was clearly intrigued. 'I was only little then.'

'Less than two years old. Once I bought you a big balloon and we tied it to the end of your bed. It was there for a long time, until the air finally all leaked out.'

Karen's brow puckered. 'It was red, wasn't it?'

Stephen laughed. 'That's right—bright red!' As if he could not help himself, he gathered his daughter into his arms and hugged her, the two dark heads very close together. Muffled in his shirtfront, Karen's voice demanded, 'Will you teach me how to ride a horse?'

'I'd love to. We'll have to get you a pony of your own, because my horse would be too big for you ... would you like to come and live with me, Karen?'

'Yes,' was the prompt reply.

'I live a very long way from here.'

'I don't care. I hate this house.'

He said carefully, 'Your mother wouldn't be living with us. I think she's decided to stay near here. Where all her friends are.'

'Could it be a brown pony?'

'Karen, do you understand what I'm saying? You'd be going up to Canada with me and leaving your mother here.'

With an almost comically adult air of explaining something that needs no explaining, Karen said, 'She couldn't leave her friends, she has such a lot of them—she's nearly always out. When will we go?'

Stephen blinked, plainly adjusting his ideas. If he had been expecting tears or a storm of protest, he could not have been more mistaken, Joanna thought drily. It would seem that Karen, with the clear eyes of the very young, had long ago seen through her mother, nor would it probably take very long for the child to focus all her affection on her father; they had made a very promising beginning already. But Stephen was speaking. '... Joanna has to go back tomorrow, but I'll have to stay for a couple of days to make certain—arrangements.' As he stood up, he picked Karen up and held her in his arms. 'Jo, would you take Karen back with you? She could use my reservation, and I'll make new ones for me. It'll take a day or two to sort out the legalities here, you see, and I'd rather Karen wasn't involved.'

What could she say? She had no choice, although with every fibre of her being she hated the idea of going back without him, hated even worse the thought of him staying here with Laura. 'Yes, of course. She could stay with me at John's. My brother has two sons, Karen, one seven years old and one ten—they live on a farm with cows and a dog and lots of barn cats.'

The grey eyes, so like Stephen's, widened with delight. 'I've never been on a farm before.'

For perhaps an hour the three of them stayed by the lily pond, Joanna effacing herself as much as possible so Stephen and Karen could get to know each other. She had perhaps never loved Stephen as much as when she saw the undisguised tenderness in his face for his little daughter, and it was impossible not to wonder if she herself would ever be granted the unimaginable happiness of giving him a child. Such a thought seemed to lead her to a blank wall. Stephen had said Laura would not be living with him—yet he had kissed her, hadn't he? And Laura, unless she was badly mistaken, was not one to give up easily.

CHAPTER TEN

THAT this was so was proved for Joanna later in the day. The three of them, she, Stephen and Karen, had gone for lunch to a fast-food place in the town of Stony Creek, at Karen's request—disposable containers, plastic cutlery, a serve-yourself atmosphere that Karen thought was delightful. 'My mother never let me come here,' she said naïvely.

Stephen grinned at Joanna, an uncomplicated smile such as he might have given a sister. 'I'm learning about this parenthood game,' he said ruefully. 'Unfortunately they have these places in Prince Edward Island as well.'

After they had eaten, they went back to Belle Maison, Stephen and Karen disappearing upstairs to pack, as Karen was to stay with them at the inn that night. Duly grateful that there was no sign of Laura, Joanna waited in the living room, sitting on the cushions in one of the bay windows idly flipping the pages of a magazine. She would be glad to leave here; she was not surprised that Karen hated the house, for it seemed designed more for display than for comfort or warmth. She couldn't help wondering what Richie had been like. . . .

'So here you are. I've been looking for you.'

Joanna jumped, for she had not heard the other woman's approach. She sat up a little straighter, purposely avoiding any of the polite, commonplace remarks she could have made.

Laura had changed into a fuchsia-coloured afternoon dress; its full skirts swirled around her admittedly excellent legs as she paced up and down like a caged tigress. 'Aren't you going to ask why I want to see you?' she demanded.

'I'm sure you'll tell me,' Joanna replied mildly.

A look like daggers. 'It's very simple. I expect you think you've won. You're going back tomorrow with Karen, and Stephen will be following in a couple of days.'

'I believe that's the arrangement.'

'Don't be too sure of it!' The bright turquoise eyes narrowed. 'The reason I brought Stephen down here in the first place was because I wanted him back—that hasn't changed.'

'I don't think I'd want a man who had divorced me.'

An angry flounce of the fuchsia skirt. 'There's such a thing as remarriage.'

Joanna responded drily, 'There's such a thing as pride, too, I would have thought.'

'I want him back!' Laura spat.

'Why, Laura? And please don't tell me you love him, because I won't believe you.'

'All right,' the other woman replied in a low, furious voice, 'I'll be honest with you. I can afford to be, because I know you're not the type to go running back to Stephen telling tales. Not that he'd believe you, anyway—he was always touchingly trusting as far as I was concerned.'

'You may not find him quite so trusting now.'

Laura laughed scornfully. 'You're just trying to frighten me. Well, it won't work. I know what I want and I'm going to get it. I want Stephen's social position. I want his money. And I want the security of marriage.'

Joanna could not help herself. 'I can understand that, Laura, because obviously you're not getting any younger. It's too bad Richie didn't come up to scratch—but then you thought you were still married to Stephen, didn't you?'

The red lips thinned, and for a moment the artfully made up face was not beautiful at all. But Laura chose to ignore Joanna's provocation. 'I have a very powerful weapon, one you don't have—I'm the mother of

Stephen's child. And he wants that child. Perhaps he'll find out that I go with the child.'

Cold fingers squeezed Joanna's heart, because what Laura had said was only too true. She, Joanna, had no comparable weapon. And she was in a horribly vulnerable position, for she loved Stephen and cared what happened to him. She said steadily, 'I don't think you realise just how much Stephen has changed since you left him. He's no longer directing a prestigious research programme. He's a part-time professor and a writer. He lives on an island several miles from a city that's nothing like Toronto. He has a beautiful house, I'll grant you that—but all his neighbours are farmers. Not at all your cup of tea, Laura.'

'Oh, we won't stay there long,' said Laura with supreme confidence. 'He could be the head of the physics department in any university across the country. Besides, I don't want you for a next-door neighbour— you make it so pitifully plain you're in love with him.'

A direct hit. Joanna raised her chin. 'Yes, I love Stephen. I love him too much to want to see him tangled up with you again, Laura, because you only love yourself. You've cheated and deceived him. You robbed him of his daughter. And now you only want to use him—you don't want him for himself at all!'

'Very touching—you have got it badly, haven't you? But it won't do you any good, you know. Because you'll fight fair, won't you? All honest and above board. Whereas I'll use any weapon I can. And I'll win.'

Joanna had had enough. She stood up, the sunlight coming through the window outlining her slim figure and her cap of chestnut hair. 'I think in this discussion we've been neglecting one very important factor.'

'What's that?' Laura's voice was sharp.

'Not what, but who ... Stephen. He's a grown man, Laura, and a good man—honest and sensitive and capable of great feeling. Four years ago you very nearly ruined his life. He'll have to decide now whether he wants to take that risk again. It's his decision, not yours or mine. He'll have to choose between us.' With a surge of confidence she saw that she had knocked Laura off balance. 'I won't lie and cheat,' she continued proudly. 'You can if you want to. If he chooses you, then I've been mistaken in him. If he chooses me . . . why, I'll be the happiest woman on earth.'

From the curving staircase in the hall came the sound of footsteps and of a child's high-pitched voice mingling with Stephen's deeper tones. Speaking quietly enough so that her voice would not carry, Laura said, 'You're leaving with him now, you and the child. But tomorrow you'll be gone and I'll be the one with Stephen. Don't count on him coming back to you, will you?'

There was supreme confidence in the magnificent turquoise eyes, confidence enough to shake Joanna's faith in her own words. She called, 'We're in here. Are you all ready, Karen?'

The child was still wearing the frilly dress, a very large teddy bear clasped under one arm. 'We're going out for dinner,' she said with an excited little skip.

Stephen looked from one woman to the other, his even gaze giving nothing away. 'You'd better say goodbye to your mother, Karen.'

In a flourish of skirts Laura sank on one knee beside the child, putting her arms around her and kissing her. 'Goodbye, Karen. Be a good girl, won't you? I'm sure I'll see you before long.' Joanna could not help watching; Karen stood like a stick, her face expressionless, and as soon as she decently could, she wriggled out of her mother's embrace.

Stephen said flatly, 'I'll see you tomorrow, Laura. Why don't I meet you at the lawyer's office at three?'

A brilliant smile, as if he had suggested a romantic rendezvous rather than an appointment with a lawyer. 'That will be fine.' With an appealing air of being unable to help herself, she reached up and kissed Stephen on the cheek, her lips lingering. 'You still use the same aftershave, don't you, darling? It brings back memories . . . I'll look forward to seeing you.'

Joanna turned away, frightened. How could she fight such a combination of beauty, assurance, and deception? She was only an ordinary girl. Certainly Stephen had called her beautiful, but under the circumstances—her mind winced away from the memory of their lovemaking—perhaps he had been less than truthful. After all, on two separate occasions he had told her Laura was the most beautiful woman he had ever seen. . . .

But Laura was addressing her. 'Goodbye, Joanna. It's been a pleasure meeting you, even if only briefly. Do have a good trip tomorrow.' The smile was dazzling.

'Thank you.' Be damned if she'd reciprocate with any of the usual polite insincerities. Finally, to her infinite relief, they had traversed the echoing hallway and were out in the sunshine again, Karen staying very close to Stephen as if afraid that at the last minute her departure would be revoked. Joanna put her in the front seat between Stephen and herself as the luggage was stowed in the trunk by the imperturbable butler. Then they were off, driving between the tall pine trees, Joanna not daring to look back.

As if he had spent every moment of the intervening four years with his daughter, Stephen began casually questioning her about her schoolwork and then her daily routine; from the artless replies emerged a picture of a child left very much to her own devices, for it soon became apparent that the priorities of both Richie and Laura had been a whirl of social activities combined with considerable travelling. Joanna marvelled that it had not soured the child's good nature. That it had not was soon apparent; what was equally apparent was that despite the opulence of Belle Maison and the expensive clothes Karen was wearing, very few treats had come her way. She was delighted with the rooms at the inn, inspecting both her father's and Joanna's, although electing to stay with her father that night, ' 'cause I'll stay with Joanna tomorrow night, won't I?' She had Stephen read the entire dinner menu to her, listening with rapt attention and selecting, to put it mildly, a somewhat unusual combination of foods that she ate with gusto. They all went for a walk after dinner, enjoying the relative cool of the dusk, Stephen carrying Karen piggyback on the way back as she was obviously flagging. She had a bath, dousing herself with Joanna's powder and skin lotion, then emerging, pink-cheeked and heavy-eyed, into Joanna's room. 'Ready, poppet?' Joanna said lightly, feeling her heart melt unexpectedly at the sight of the child, so like Stephen. 'We'll have to go through the corridor to your father's room.'

They tapped on Stephen's door and he let them in. It was a room very like Joanna's, although with masculine appurtenances scattered around rather than feminine. A cot had been set up along one wall, Karen's teddy bear already perched on the pillow, surveying them through unwinking glass eyes, his embroidered mouth in a permanently benign smile. Karen clutched him to her. 'Goodnight, Joanna.' She yawned, adding without a trace of selfconsciousness, 'Goodnight, Daddy.'

An emotion Joanna could not have defined passed briefly across Stephen's face. He bent and kissed his daughter. 'Sleep well, dear.' Tucking the covers around her, he added, 'I'm just going to take Joanna to her room, and then I'll be back. Will the light bother you if I sit in the corner and read?' A sleepy shake of the head. 'Okay—I won't be a minute.'

He walked the short distance down the thickly carpeted corridor with Joanna. Unable to think of a thing to say, she unlocked her door and turned to face him. He ushered her into the room, partly closing the door behind him. 'Well, Joanna . . .' he said heavily. 'Last night seems a very long time ago, doesn't it?' He rubbed his brow with his fingers. 'I can hardly believe that after all this time my daughter is in the next room and that tomorrow you'll be taking her home with you ... I wish I were going, too.'

'So do I.' She spoke more vehemently than she would have wished to.

'I have to stay, Jo. I want Karen in my legal custody, and I want to make sure it's done right. It may take three or four days.' He gave Joanna his rare, heart-stopping smile. 'I know she'll be in good hands—better hands than she has been. Although I still find it hard to believe how calmly she's left her mother.'

'I think her mother is virtually a stranger to Karen,' Joanna said with a careful lack of emphasis.

'You may be right.' Again he rubbed at his brow.

'Do you have a headache?'

'I think I'm still in a state of shock. The last person I expected to see when I walked into that house was Laura.'

'Yes. ...' Her voice was little more than a whisper, not that Stephen noticed, for he was sunk in his own thoughts.

'It was as though the past was happening all over again ... she was wearing a grey dress very like the one she had on this morning the first time I saw her. ...'

'But that was eight years ago, Stephen—a great deal has happened since then,' said Joanna with deliberate matter-of-factness.

'Yes. You're right, of course. Sorry Jo, I'm not making much sense, am I? This has been one hell of a day ... I probably won't be long following Karen's example and going to bed.'

Joanna stood very still, aching for him to make some further reference to their lovemaking last night to show that it had been real for him, not a dream or a passing fancy just as quickly forgotten. But all he said was, 'I hope you'll sleep well, Joanna. Why don't we meet for breakfast at eight-thirty? That'll give us lots of time to get to the airport.'

She would not cry, she would not. . . . 'Fine,' she said brightly. 'Goodnight, Stephen.'

'Goodnight. I—oh, hell!' He gave her a quick, hard kiss on the lips and then he was gone, the door shutting decisively behind him. Joanna flipped the lock and put the chain in place. Then she undressed, carefully hanging up her clothes despite the fact that tomorrow they were going to be folded in her suitcase, then slipping on her nightdress and cleaning her teeth. None of these actions required any thought. It was only when she got into bed and turned out the light that thought and emotion attacked her, twin foes. If it had been a different room, a different bed, it might have been easier. But only last night in this very bed Stephen's hands and mouth and body had assailed and delighted her, carrying her irrevocably across the boundary that lay between innocence and knowledge. Loving him as she did, she had given him generously all that was hers to give; now, as she lay on her back staring up into the semi-darkness, she couldn't help wondering what it had meant to him. Had it been merely a means of oblivion, a way of forgetting that in a few short hours he was to see the house where Laura had lived and, so he had thought at the time, died? Had it been simply desire? A need to satisfy animal hunger too long held in abeyance? And why should he not have satisfied them, she thought bitterly, when she herself was there, so obviously willing?

Turning on her stomach, she buried her face in the pillow in a vain effort to shut out the images that haunted her: Stephen's naked body hovering over hers, his grey eyes intent on her love-flushed face; Laura's exquisite features appealing to Stephen for understanding, inevitably reminding him of other nights in another bed, and of the body, now so slim and supple, that had once borne him a child . . . round and round the faces circled in her tired brain, Stephen, Laura, Karen, herself, all inextricably entangled. Yet as the slow

minutes passed, it began to seem to Joanna that of all
four of them she was the outsider, the one who did not
belong. The other three were bound together by past
history and by ties of blood. But not she. She was the
newcomer on the scene. The friend. The girl next door.
But not the woman Stephen loved. . . .

In the lobby of the inn the old grandfather clock had
struck two o'clock before Joanna finally fell asleep. But
she was disturbed by nightmares and it was not until
dawn that her body stilled and she slept the deep sleep
of exhaustion. The knocking on her door had been
going on for some time before she awoke, with a
sensation of dragging herself up from immense depths
to surface in a world of grey light and rain running
down the windowpane. Standing up, she pulled on her
housecoat and went to the door. Stephen and Karen,
both fully dressed, were standing in the corridor.
'What's the time?' Joanna muttered.

'Eight-thirty.'

She rubbed her eyes. 'Oh, lord . . . I'd better get
ready. Give me ten minutes. Better still, why don't I
meet you in the dining room?'

A hand fell on her shoulder. In her confused state
after the long hours of the night the contact was
unbearable, the warmth and weight of his hand too
poignant a reminder of something she wanted to forget.
She stepped back and the hand dropped to his side. Not
looking at him, her own face pale and set, she repeated,
'Ten minutes,' and quickly locked the door.

It was nearer twenty minutes before Joanna crossed
the lobby to the dining room. She had showered and
washed her hair and made up her face, putting on the
attractive linen suit she had travelled in on the way
down, with dangling gold earrings and very high heels.
A group of men waiting in the lobby eyed her with
approval, while the head waiter gave her something
more than his usual professional smile, both little
occurrences doing a world of good to her rather

battered ego. So as she was escorted through the tables to the one where Stephen and Karen were already seated, there was a smile on her face. 'Good morning,' she said cheerfully, making a great play of consulting her watch. 'I'm only twenty-five minutes late—that's not bad.' As Stephen opened his mouth to reply, she forestalled him. 'And no sexist remarks about women always being late! How are you, Karen? Did you sleep well?'

As the meal progressed Joanna purposely kept the conversation on a lighthearted level; inwardly she knew how much she was dreading the separation from Stephen, sensing that to keep him at a distance was the only way she could deal with it. Although the terrors of the night had retreated, she was nevertheless left with the conviction that her love for Stephen was unrequited; not for anything was she going to let him see that she hated leaving him with Laura. So she talked and laughed and joked until finally, thank God, they were at the airport, waiting at the gate to board the aircraft. Karen had gone to the window, pressing her little nose to the pane as she watched a sleek silver jet taxi across the runway. Stephen said urgently, 'Joanna, what's wrong?'

'Wrong? Nothing's wrong. Don't worry about Karen, Stephen, I'll take good care of her.'

'I'm not at all worried about Karen, because I know she's in the best of hands.' He took her by the arm and must have felt her muscles tense in rejection. 'You're different this morning, Jo, I can't seem to get near you. What's the matter?'

Her smile was patently false. 'You're imagining things.'

'Damn it, I'm not!' His fingers tightened around her sleeve.

Over the loudspeaker their flight number was called, pre-boarding for passengers with young children. 'We have to go, Stephen,' said Joanna with such transparent relief that he gave her a shake.

'I hate leaving you like this! Look, I'll be back in three or four days at the most—I'll give you a call tomorrow to let you know what's up.'

Karen had run back to them, tugging at Joanna's hand. 'It's time to go! Goodbye, Daddy!'

He swung the child up into his arms, kissing her soundly. 'Goodbye, love. Be a good girl for Joanna and I'll see you in a few days.' Then he put her down, perhaps seeing out of the corner of his eye how Joanna was edging her way round them. 'Come here, Jo.'

'Stephen, I——'

'Come here.'

Impossible to argue with that tone of voice, nor in her heart of hearts, despite all her brave resolutions, did she want to. She took a step towards him and felt herself gathered in his arms, held so close to him that muscle and bone imprinted themselves on her memory and she trembled with weakness. Blindly she raised her face for his kiss; it seared through her body, and when he released her, her eyes were brilliant with unshed tears. 'Joanna——'

'We must go. Come on, Karen.' Almost running, she hurried the child to the gate, holding out their boarding passes to the attendant. Karen was waving at her father over her shoulder; Joanna did not look back. Only when she had walked down the carpeted corridor to the door of the plane did she begin, fractionally, to relax. But then Karen's ingenuous, 'Why are you crying, Joanna?' knocked her off balance again.'

'I'm not——' she began. Then she gave the child a watery smile. 'Yes, I am. I guess I just hate goodbyes, Karen. Silly, isn't it?'

'Maybe you'll marry my daddy,' Karen said hopefully.

Horrified, Joanna whispered, 'Oh, no—you mustn't think that!'

'Why not? He kissed you.' It was plainly a logical progression of events to Karen.

'Because—oh, I can't explain, Karen. Your father and I are good friends, that's all. Here, these are our seats. You go by the window so you can look out. Let me buckle your seat belt.'

It took them a minute or two to get settled, by which time Karen's attention was glued to the window, where a baggage cart was trundling by and another plane was being waved in to the next gate. Joanna did up her own seat belt and leaned her head back, closing her eyes, her one desire for the plane to leave and put as many miles as possible between her and Stephen.

CHAPTER ELEVEN

IT was a long day. Fortunately Karen slept on the flight from Boston to Halifax, and fortunately also they made all their connections with no delays. John and the boys were at the Charlottetown airport to meet them, for Joanna had phoned ahead from Halifax; when she saw the two boys, Karen was struck dumb with shyness, a rather touching demonstration of how much of her life had been spent in adult company. As they waited at the carrousel for their baggage, Karen standing very close to Joanna, John said with a casual air that did not deceive Joanna at all, 'I have to come to the airport again tomorrow. Sally's arriving on the afternoon flight.'

'Oh, John!' She hugged him fiercely. 'I'm so glad. That's sooner than you expected, isn't it?'

'Yeah—apparently she's made fantastic progress this last week.'

'Goodness, I'm glad I got back today. That'll give me time to get everything ready tomorrow.' She was genuinely happy for both of them, and somehow this eased some of the hurt that had been lodged like a hard lump inside her all day. She began talking to the boys, describing some of the things she had seen in North Carolina and gradually drawing Karen into the conversation, amused to see how Brian adopted a kind of protective, older-brother attitude towards the little girl almost immediately. By the time they reached the farm Karen's shyness had vanished, and it was only with difficulty that Joanna restrained her from wanting an immediate tour of all the barns and fields; the fact that it was dark did not seem to discourage Karen at all. 'Tomorrow,' Joanna said firmly. 'Right now it's bedtime. If you get up early in the morning you can watch John milk the cow, and maybe Brian will have a minute before he goes to school to show you where the barn cats live, and how to gather the eggs.'

Thus appeased, Karen went to bed without further protest and five minutes later was fast asleep. The boys were soon settled, and John made a pot of tea, which Joanna carried into the living room. Sinking down on the chesterfield, she pulled off her shoes with a sigh of relief, giving her brother a quick smile. 'Nice to be home, John. And thanks for meeting us.'

'You're welcome. But you look tired, Sis—tell me what went on down there. Why didn't Stephen come back with you?'

Picking her words, she gave him a carefully edited version of the past three days, taking a malicious pleasure in describing Belle Maison, and then telling how Laura had been there to meet them.

'Good heavens! Who sent the telegram, then?'

'She did.' Briefly, her voice devoid of expression, she repeated Laura's justification for her actions.

John gave a long, low whistle. 'She sounds like a lady to avoid. What does she look like?'

'Gorgeous,' Joanna said miserably. 'Absolutely gorgeous. She's got these big blue eyes and if she told you black was white, you'd believe her.'

'Hmm . . . so is that why Stephen's still there?'

'He stayed there to get legal custody of Karen; he and Laura had an appointment with the lawyer this afternoon. But she wants him back, John, she told me she did.' Her voice quivered. 'I'm scared he'll bring her up here, to live with him.'

John said gently, 'And you're head-over-heels in love with him, aren't you?'

'Is it that obvious?'

'I know you pretty well, Sis. I think it was inevitable from the first moment you saw him. He's a very different proposition from Drew.'

'He's not in love with me,' she blurted, and there was no need to say that she was not referring to Drew.

'I wouldn't be so sure about that.'

'John, he's not! I think he's still in love with Laura, no matter what she's done.'

'He couldn't be . . . come on, Jo, you're overtired and you're imagining the worst. I think you should get to bed and catch up on your sleep, and everything will look better in the morning.'

'Maybe you're right.' Her smile was almost convincing. 'I feel better for having told someone, anyway.'

'Of course I'm right. Now off to bed with you.'

Buoyed up by John's optimism, Joanna slept soundly, and the next day she was too busy to sit around and worry about Stephen and Laura. She gave the whole house a quick vacuuming, prepared a special dinner of all Sally's favourites, and picked lilac and tulips to decorate the house; and all day she was careful to keep an eye on Karen, anxious that the child settle in well. She need not have worried. Brian had shown Karen the barn and the sandpit; arrayed in cast-offs of Marks,' jeans and a T-shirt that were too large but nevertheless more suitable than the dresses that were all that seemed to be in her suitcase, Karen spent most of the day outdoors. After lunch John left on the bus to go to the airport, as Sally would have to travel by ambulance; the boys came home from school and went outside to play, soon joined by Lisette from next door. Through the kitchen window Joanna was amused to notice how at first the two little girls circled rather warily around each other, and then suddenly decided to be friends; a very noisy game of tag ensued.

It was nearly suppertime when the ambulance turned up the driveway. Joanna went outside, wiping her hands on her apron. Followed by Karen, the two boys came running down the hill. Then, suddenly shy of their own mother, they hung back.

The driver jumped out, went round to the back of the

ambulance, and with John's help lowered Sally into a wheelchair. John carefully pushed it up the driveway as the ambulance reversed down the hill; Sally was sitting up very straight, the afternoon sun glinting in her dark brown hair, her face, thinner than Joanna remembered it, flushed with excitement. John stopped the chair near the two boys.

Sally and Joanna exchanged a quick glance of perfect understanding that said without words, the boys come first, we'll talk later. Then Sally said calmly, 'Don't be frightened by the wheelchair, boys. I'm able to walk, but not on rough ground yet. Brian, you've grown at least two inches! And Mark, haven't you lost another tooth?'

As if to prove her point Mark gave his gap-toothed grin, and suddenly everyone was laughing and the two boys clustered around the wheelchair, their mother's arms around them. 'It's lovely to see you both again,' Sally gulped. 'Oh dear, I swore I wouldn't cry—it's because I'm so happy. Brian, what did you do to your chin?'

'I fell off my bike.'

As John began pushing the wheelchair towards the house, Joanna and Karen hung back a little, Joanna feeling oddly redundant: from now until bedtime Sally would be getting reacquainted with her sons, and then she and John would become instantly absorbed in each other, in a private world designed for two, not three.

She was exaggerating a little, because everyone gathered in the kitchen, all except Sally taking part in the preparations for the meal. At first Karen had a tendency to stand back, watching big-eyed as the boys and their mother bantered back and forth; however, before long even she was gathered into the family circle, insisting on sitting between Brian and Joanna at the big pine table. After the dishes were washed and the boys had done their homework, they all joined in a riotous game of cards, until John said finally, 'Last hand, boys—your mother's getting tired.'

'I *am* tired,' Sally confessed ruefully. 'But it's so lovely to be home again—you can't imagine . . . you'd better go and get your pyjamas on, boys. You too, Karen. Then come downstairs and say goodnight.' As the three of them raced for the staircase she turned to Joanna. 'She's a sweet little girl, but very quiet for her age. I don't think she quite knows what to make of us all.'

'Neither would you if you'd had her upbringing,' Joanna said feelingly. 'I shouldn't imagine she's ever experienced any of the give and take of a normal family.'

'When I was hugging the boys I saw her watching as if I was doing something extraordinary.'

'Her mother is a cold-blooded and manipulative woman who cares for no one but herself,' Joanna said succinctly.

'I see. . . .'

Joanna blushed, adding lamely and unnecessarily, 'I didn't like her.'

As if to punctuate her remarks, the telephone shrilled in the hall and there was the thud of footsteps coming down the stairs. 'I'll get it!' Brian yelled.

Joanna sat immobile, certain that it was Stephen; she had been carrying around with her all day the anticipation that he would phone. She heard Brian say, 'Karen's right here—Karen, it's your dad,' and then Karen's excited chatter as she began to describe the farm, the animals, Sally's return, and what they had had for dinner. Joanna was unaware of the tension in her features as she waited, unaware of her fingers restlessly plucking at the folds of her skirt. Although she was certain that he would ask to speak to her, she had no idea of what she was going to say when he did, because all she could think of was the time he must have spent with Laura since she, Joanna, had seen him last. . . . How had it affected him? Somehow she doubted that she would have the courage to ask.

Finally Karen poked her head around the door. 'Daddy wants to speak to you, Joanna.'

Joanna got up hastily, wishing the telephone was in a more private location, knowing from experience that every word would carry into the kitchen. Taking the receiver from Karen, she said warily, 'Hello.'

'Joanna? Speak up, I can hardly hear you.'

His brusqueness threw her further off balance. 'How are you?'

He said impatiently, 'I'm going to have to stay here for at least another three or four days—a few complications have come up, but I don't want to go into them on the phone. Will Karen be all right with you?'

'Yes, she's fine . . . complications?'

'She told me Sally's back.'

I don't want to talk about Sally, Joanna thought rebelliously, I want to talk about you and me. 'Yes, she got home today. It's lovely to have her back.'

'Karen seems very taken with the whole family, especially Brian. I heard a lot of Brian says this and Brian says that.' Joanna could think of no reply to this. 'Are you still there?' he demanded. 'This is a terrible connection, a lot of noise on the wires. Listen, Joanna, as soon as I can give you a definite day of arrival, I'll phone again. How long before you have to go back to work?'

'I have another week of holidays.'

'I'll surely be finished up by then,' he said grimly. 'I really do appreciate all you're doing for me and Karen—the child's far better off up there than down here, I'm convinced of it.'

Joanna had had enough of this innocuous conversation, so full of things unsaid. 'I'd better go,' she said coolly. 'It's the children's bedtime and Sally's looking very tired herself.'

'All right.' He added abruptly, 'The telephone can be a damned frustrating means of communication, don't you agree? Take care of yourself, Jo, and I promise I'll be home within the week.'

Is it still home? she wanted to ask. But before she could, he had said goodbye and the connection had been cut with a finality that absurdly made her want to cry. She stared at the receiver with something like hatred. The only thing he had said that she could relate to was that the telephone could be very frustrating—with that she would agree. As for the rest, lodged in her mind was that one little phrase about the complications. What had he meant by that? Legal complications? Or emotional complications? The one person's name he had not mentioned was Laura's; in her overwrought state the omission seemed horribly significant.

From the kitchen John called, 'Can we get these three to bed, Sis?'

Pulling herself together, she put her head around the kitchen door. The first thing she saw was John standing very close to Sally's wheelchair, his hand on her shoulder as he smiled down at her. It was only a smile. But there was something in the quality of it, in the shining happiness behind it, that made her remember with a pang of sheer agony how Stephen had smiled at her after he had made love to her. How long ago it seemed, almost as though it had happened to another woman. And after that abortive conversation, how far away he seemed, a distance that had very little to do with miles.

Pasting a bright smile on her face, she said, 'Ready, you three? Upstairs with you!'

The final straw came when Karen put her arms around Joanna's neck and hugged her, saying sleepily, 'I like Brian's mother. I think you should be my mother.'

Joanna stiffened. She bit her lip, trying to think of the right thing to say. With attempted lightness she murmured, 'Your father might have something to say about that, Karen. Sleep well, won't you, dear?' The endearment slipped out in spite of her; the child's resemblance to Stephen was a constant reminder of him.

It was a reminder Joanna could have done without as the days dragged by. On the positive side Sally grew a little stronger each day, and it was heartwarming to see the family reunited; John went about his work whistling, a spring in his step. Karen had settled into life on the farm as if she had been born to it, and try as she might it was impossible for Joanna not to become more and more fond of the child, both for herself as well as for her relationship to Stephen. That the attachment was mutual was easily to be seen; it was all there in the way Karen tucked her hand in Joanna's when they walked up to the barn, and kissed her goodnight at bedtime. More and more as the days passed Joanna was convinced she should be discouraging this attachment, for deep within her, fed by fear and uncertainty, was the conviction that Stephen would not return from North Carolina alone. He would bring Laura with him, and for Karen the blissful days at the farm would be over.

When he phoned for the second time, she was out riding; Sally gave her the message that he would be returning the following evening. Karen was delighted. Joanna, for all her outward composure, was panic-stricken. The one night they had spent together they had shared an intimacy greater than any she could have envisaged; but since then he had become a stranger. She had no idea whether he regretted that night or even thought about it at all, no idea what his feelings were towards her—or towards Laura. He was an enigma. Yet despite all this, she still loved him. The bond that bound her to him could not be destroyed by absence or rationalised out of existence. Deeply rooted in her psyche, it was as much a part of her as her love for her brother and his family. She was, in effect, a prisoner.

On the day he was to arrive she indulged in an orgy

of cleaning and baking and ironing, a whirl of activity that Sally watched with a faint, understanding smile. John had not told her the exact hour of Stephen's arrival, nor did she want to know it, for the hours passed slowly enough as it was, without her having to count minutes. As it happened the rest of the family were in the living room when the black Mercedes came up the driveway and the tap came at the back door. Taking a deep breath, she opened the door.

As if it belonged to someone else, her brain recorded a quick series of impressions. He was alone. Even standing a step below her, he was taller than she. He was wearing a light raincoat over his business suit, and he looked very tired. To her horror, because she had meant to be cool and detached, she heard herself say, 'Where's Laura?'

'Laura? What the hell do you mean?'

It was not a propitious beginning. 'Is she in the car?'

'For God's sake! As far as I know she's in that misnamed architectural horror in North Carolina. You surely didn't expect me to bring her here?'

'I—I didn't know what you were going to do.'

'Believe me, that's the last thing I'd do. Where's Karen?'

Belatedly recalling her manners, Joanna stood aside so he could come in, and as he did so, Karen came racing into the room. She looked very different from the prim and proper little girl in the frilly dress whom he had last seen at the airport; her hair was pulled back in pigtails, and she was wearing hand-me-downs of Mark's. 'Hi, Daddy!' she shrieked, flinging herself at him as he knelt to greet her.

Joanna turned away, her thoughts in a turmoil. He had not brought Laura—that much was clear. Had not even wanted to bring her. But the relief this should have engendered was clouded by other considerations, for when she had opened the door for him, he had not looked happy: he had looked exhausted, like a man at the end of his tether. Something had happened to him in North Carolina, she was sure of it. But what?

Karen was pulling him into the living room where the others were, and slowly Joanna followed, conscious primarily of a sense of anticlimax. She had been steeling herself for this meeting for days. Now it was over, and virtually nothing had happened.

He stayed for over an hour, some of the strain in his face relaxing as he joined in the family chatter and as Karen so obviously showed her pleasure at seeing him. Finally he said, 'We'd better get going, Karen. Are your things packed?'

'Up in my room. I'll show you.'

They came downstairs a few minutes later, Stephen with the suitcases, Karen with her teddy bear, and made their goodbyes. Joanna accompanied them to the back door, where Karen gave her a fierce hug. ' 'Bye, Jo. I can come over here for visits, can't I?'

'Of course you can,' Stephen intervened. 'Although maybe not tomorrow—I thought we'd go into Charlottetown and get you some clothes and some bedroom furniture. Would you like that?'

'Jeans like Brian and Mark wear?'

'I guess so,' Stephen agreed ruefully. He looked over at Joanna, who was standing quietly by the door, one hand resting on the frame. The overhead light caught gleams of copper in her hair, although her eyes, in shadow, were unreadable. He said with obvious sincerity, 'Thank you, Joanna.' He glanced down at his daughter. 'From both me and Karen. It was much better that she be here for the past week rather than with me. It was . . . difficult, to say the least.'

'Yes?'

'Yes.' He added abruplty, 'I'll tell you about it later.'

Tell me about what? she wondered. About Laura? She answered noncommittally, 'I go back to work the day after tomorrow. But I'll be out here as much as I can until Sally's feeling stronger.'

His eyes searched her face. 'You're so different from Laura—or so I hope. Sometimes I hardly know what I believe any more.'

For the first time that evening the real Joanna showed through. 'I *am* different,' she blazed, her chin tilted defiantly.

His voice was so low Karen could not have heard him. 'I hope to God you are.'

For a moment there was desperation in the steel-grey eyes and instinctively Joanna touched his sleeve. 'What's wrong?'

'We can't talk now. Another time—I'll be in touch. Do you have everything, Karen? Get the outside door for us, would you, Jo?'

She had to pass him, so close that her shirt brushed against his raincoat. Flipping on the outside light, she pushed the screen door open and held it wide. Karen and the teddy bear jumped down the step. Stephen paused briefly. Like a man who could not help himself he bent his head and kissed her, only the lightest touch of his lips on hers before he drew back and followed Karen down the step. Very slowly Joanna let the door close, hearing the crunch of their footsteps in the dirt driveway, the slam of the car doors, the purr of the motor. The beams of the headlights picked out the barn and the tall lilac bushes before gradually diminishing in strength as the car reversed down the driveway. Only when she could no longer hear it or see it did she go back into the kitchen. Something was wrong, that much was certain. Something had happened to Stephen during the past few days, and she would be willing to bet it was related to Laura, cold, beautiful Laura.

As she put away the last of the saucepans, her mouth was set in a way John would have recognised and been duly wary of. Whatever had happened, Laura was no longer on the scene; whereas she, Joanna, definitely was. And Stephen needed her, she was convinced of it. It was only a question of waiting until he came to her. . . .

CHAPTER TWELVE

BRAVE words. But as the June days passed and summer finally emerged from under the mantle of spring, Joanna was to wonder over and over again if she had misread the whole situation, if her intuitive conviction that Stephen needed her was not totally false. He did not appear to need her, for he made no move to speak to her privately or even to see her alone. She saw him—that was inevitable, for Rajah was still in John's stables, and Karen played with the boys and Lisette every chance she got. But always there were other people around, noise and confusion and laughter, as effective a barrier between them as a high brick wall would have been or a barbed wire fence. She could not accuse him of being unfriendly or rude; he was simply distant, an infinitely long way away, as if that one magical night had never occurred, had merely been a dream or a fantasy.

He did not need her. He did not love her. Inescapably these were the conclusions she came to.

There was another, added, conclusion, springing from her knowledge of what Laura had done to him in the past. It began to seem increasingly likely to her that Stephen might never love a woman again or be able to say to anyone those three simple little words, I love you. He had loved and trusted Laura, and she had thrown it all back in his face. She had left him a cripple, a man maimed at the very roots of his being.

Because Joanna was a direct and honest creature, faced for the first time in her life with a situation she could not alter, she suffered. It was being borne upon her that one cannot create love where it does not exist. She could have forced some kind of a confrontation with Stephen, she supposed, but what good would it

172

have done? If he did not want to talk to her, or touch her, or make love to her, if he found it impossible to love her as she had so foolishly admitted to loving him, what good would it do to talk to him? None whatsoever. It would only cause her pain, and no doubt embarrass him.

So whenever possible she began to absent herself at times when she thought he might appear, and in this she was helped by her work, for she was back on the evening shift and regular call nights. But she could not always be gone, and gradually the pleasure of seeing him, of simply being in the same room with him, began to be outweighed by the pain.

It was well over ten days after his return that Joanna overheard a conversation between Stephen and Karen that seemed to distil the misery and frustration of all those hours into one unbearably poignant moment. She was in the barn one evening, bent over in Star's stall cleaning the mare's back hooves with the pick, when she heard the barn door open and the sound of voices, Stephen's and Karen's.

'Can I give him the carrot, Daddy?'

She had two choices: to show herself and speak to them, or to remain where she was, out of sight, until they had gone. Rajah's stall was separated from Star's by an untidy pile of hay bales, and unless they actually came over to pat Star, they would never see her. Her body tense as she knelt in the straw, she waited for them to leave.

'Here, let me lift you up.' Stephen's deep voice.

'His nose is so soft, like velvet.' To Joanna's ears came the sound of chewing as Rajah demolished the carrot. 'He's got big teeth.'

'Rub his forehead—he likes that.'

A pause. 'When will my pony arrive?'

'The workmen at our place told me today they should finish the first stall tomorrow. So we could probably pick her up the day after.'

Joanna had a kink in her knee. She shifted slightly, moving her face to avoid the swish of Star's tail. Karen said raptly, 'And you'll teach me how to ride?'

'Sure I will.'

'I *am* glad I came here to live! It's much more fun.'

Knowing him as she did, Joanna picked up the emotion underlying Stephen's words. 'I'm glad you did too, sweetheart. Although I worried about you missing your mother.'

'She was never home anyway.' No bitterness in Karen's tone, only an almost adult acceptance. 'She's pretty and she smells nice and wears lovely clothes, but you couldn't hug her ... not like you can hug Jo, f'r instance.'

'. . . oh?'

'Jo's nice. You're nice too, Daddy.' Risking a glance through a knothole, Joanna saw Karen put her arms around her father's neck, nuzzling her face into his. 'I do love you.'

She saw something constrict in Stephen's face. His arms tightened around the child. 'I love you too, Karen.'

Joanna sank back in the straw, leaning her face against Star's smooth, warm flank. For a horrifying instant she was jealous of Karen, who had Stephen's arms around her and Stephen's voice telling her he loved her. Jealous of Stephen's daughter, a six-year-old child ... sickened by her own reaction, she closed her eyes, and from a long way away heard Karen say, 'Your sweater is as soft as Rajah's nose. Let's go down to the house and see Jo.'

A fractional hesitation that spoke volumes to the listening girl. 'All right.' There was the sound of Stephen's footsteps on the floorboards, the squeal of the barn door on its hinges, and then silence.

Not even stopping to think, Joanna picked up Star's blanket and saddle and threw them across the mare's back, smoothing the pad and tightening the girth. Star took the bit delicately between her teeth. Joanna buckled the bridle and grabbed the reins, leading the mare out of the far door, the one that faced away from the house. Hidden from view, she swung herself up in the saddle and adjusted the girth, then squeezed Star's sides with her heels. 'Let's go, girl,' she murmured, guiding the mare straight up behind the barn into the woods, where she could pick up the trail that led to the beach. She needed to be by the sea. That much she knew.

It was not the best of times for a ride. Evening was drawing in early, for the sky was heavily overcast, the purple-fringed clouds torn by the wind. She and Star were sheltered among the trees, but the top branches were swaying back and forth with a sound like the waves on the shore. A storm had been forecast, Joanna knew. She spurred Star on, wanting to reach the shore while it was still light, the weather suiting her mood. She hated herself for that quick stab of jealousy, hated herself for resenting Karen even for an instant. The child had had little enough love in her short life; how could she begrudge her Stephen's love?

The answer was, of course, simple. Because she herself wanted to be loved by Stephen. He could say, 'I love you', to Karen. He either could not, or did not want to, say it to Joanna. Which it was, she had no idea. She only knew it had hurt her unbearably to hear him admit his love for his daughter. Irrational, certainly. Ungenerous, also. Oh, damn, damn, damn. . . .

The mare shied as a dead limb snapped from a tree, and Joanna brought her attention back to her riding. A drop of rain stung her face. She frowned, for she did not want to turn back, not before she had exorcised her inner confusion in a mad gallop along the beach. As she and Star emerged from the trees into the field that sloped to the shoreline, the full force of the gale flailed at the mare's mane and tail, slicing through Joanna's thin sweater.

Even the sheltered waters of the bay were being driven against the rocks in a grey-white churn of foam, while from the open ocean came the constant, thunderous roar of giant breakers. Black-tipped wings held stiffly, a gull whipped through the air above them.

Joanna drew a deep breath of the damp, salt-laden air. The tide was low enough that despite the waves there was a long stretch of open sand, and she leaned forward, patting Star's neck. 'Let's go!' she yelled. At a trot they crossed the flattened grass of the field, where the wildflowers bowed before the wind. Then there was sand under Star's hooves, and as if the mare had caught some of Joanna's recklessness, she broke into a gallop. The dunes flashed by. The waves threw themselves onto the beach, hissing and seething in retreat. Breathless and exhilarated, Joanna crouched low in the saddle, hearing the thud of hooves and the whistling of the wind in her ears, her vision restricted to the dull green of the eel grass, the pale yellow sand, the grey waters of the bay. Wind, water, sand, and the sheer joy of motion . . . there was nothing else in the world.

They came to the channel that separated them from the island. Not even stopping to think of the storm or of the approach of darkness, Joanna slowed Star to a trot and urged her forward. Water splashing around her legs, the mare surged through the whirling currents, faltering only momentarily where a shelf of sand had been carved away and the sea came up to her belly. Then she was scrambling up the slope on to the dry sand and they were galloping the length of the island.

They passed the single outcrop of sandstone and the crown of stunted spruce trees, and it was not until they reached the far end that Joanna brought the mare to a halt. Sliding to the ground and clasping the reins in her hand, she stood still, awed by the majesty of the scene in front of her. The island jutted out into the bay, whose narrow opening to the sea was directly ahead of her. One after the other, massive and inexorable, the ocean waves reared up into the air, the spume blown from their crests before they crashed on the sand bar in a mad tumble of foam. The noise was deafening, the uncontrolled power of the ocean, even at a distance, terrifying. Yet there was something so fundamental, so real, in this display of nature's might that Joanna was unable to move, almost hypnotised by the constant movement of clouds and water and the ceaseless roar of the waves. She had no idea how much time passed. She only gradually came to her senses because the cold was seeping through her clothes, making her shiver, and the rain had begun in earnest.

Giving herself a shake, she said out loud, 'Star, we're crazy. We'd better go home—it's nearly dark and I'm freezing!' She mounted, and with the wind behind them, they began trotting down the beach. Just as suddenly as Joanna had been seized by the urge to come down to the beach, she found herself wishing she was home again, in the lamplit warmth of the kitchen with the coffee pot bubbling on the stove. She must have been mad to have gone so far on such a wild night. And John and Sally would have missed her by now, would be wondering where on earth she had gone.

Unconsciously she must have been squeezing Star's sides with her legs, because the mare had gallantly responded with a canter. It seemed to take a long time to reach the far end of the island, where the channel was a dark, and surely much wider, ribbon between the two strips of pale sand. They wheeled in a circle while Joanna examined it, inwardly berating herself for her own stupidity. The tide was on the rise; subconsciously she had known that. Why then had she delayed so long watching the waves?

She had no choice but to try and cross the channel, for the only alternative was to spend the night on the island, a prospect that made her shudder with more than the cold. Once more she wheeled Star in a circle before heading her straight for the channel. And then, with fiendish mistiming, disaster struck.

It was only afterwards that Joanna was able to piece together exactly what had happened: that a small, dead spruce tree had been torn loose from its moorings by the gale and had swept across the empty beach straight for the mare, an anonymous dark shape that must have seemed to have had a life of its own. At the time all she knew was that Star suddenly reared, flinging herself sideways. The reins were torn from Joanna's hands. Thrown off balance, she felt herself begin to fall and instinctively kicked her feet free of the stirrups. Her body hit the sand with a thud, knocking the breath from her lungs. Dimly she heard Star's whicker of panic as the tangled grey branches caught at her hooves. Then the mare was splashing into the sea, her nostrils flaring and her eyes wild as she forged the surging waters of the channel.

Joanna shoved herself upright and stumbled to her feet. 'Star—come back!' But the mare was beyond reason. She had hauled herself up on the sand on the other side and was galloping down the beach, a rapidly diminishing figure soon swallowed up in the darkness.

Joanna stared after her, momentarily oblivious of the rain that lashed at her back. Star was gone, and she was alone on the island. Scarcely thinking, she ran down to the water's edge and waded in. But almost instantly it came over the tops of her boots, soaking her jodhpurs, icy cold. She retreated back on to the sand. She was trapped. . . .

Belatedly she began to think. Surely Star would follow all her instincts and head for the house, for the familiar barn and stable. Then John would know his sister had got herself into yet another scrape and would come looking for her. Or would send Stephen. Oh, *why* had she been so stupid?

She was trembling, both from the delayed shock of her fall and from the cold, for her sweater was soaked through. Her boots squelching with every step, she headed for the outcrop of eroded red sandstone that merged with the sand well above the water's edge; it would provide at least a modicum of shelter from the wind and rain. Tucking herself under a ledge, she hugged her knees in a vain effort to warm herself and tried to review her situation in a calm and rational manner.

Her immediate surroundings were not conducive to comfort. Water dripped from the ledge, while the soft, crumbling rock smelled unpleasant. Her clothing was wet through. The gathering darkness was full of strange sounds, rustles and creaks that must surely emanate from the spruces, overriding the constant splash and gurgle of the sea. But she was, essentially, in no immediate danger. For one thing the crest of the island was well above the high tide mark. For another, John knew of her predilection for mad gallops on the beach, so that this would be the first place he would think of looking. Nevertheless, she would be causing them concern, and worry was the last thing Sally needed.

Her thoughts going round and round in circles, she waited, trying not to jump at every noise. Her teeth were chattering. She tried standing up and walking around in an effort to get warm, but the rain only made her wetter and the wind seemed to chill her to the bone, so she soon huddled back in her shelter again.

Although in some ways it seemed for ever, it could not actually have been that long before she saw at the far end of the beach the bright yellow beam of a flashlight scanning the sand. She stood up, forgetting about the ledge and scraping her cheekbone, the sharp pain bringing tears to her eyes. Dashing them away, she screamed at the top of her lungs, 'I'm up here—on the island!'

The wind tore the words from her mouth. Knowing it was useless to call again until her unknown rescuer was much closer, she helplessly watched his slow progress up the beach; he must have seen Star, and realised that the mare was wet from more than the rain, and it was for that reason that he was searching the shoreline, perhaps even afraid that Star's rider had drowned. . . .

Eventually he was close enough that Joanna's initial suspicion was confirmed: behind the bright circle of light loomed the bulk of a big black horse. Rajah. So the rider would have to be Stephen.

She tried again, cupping her hands around her mouth and filling her lungs with air, before yelling his name into the darkness. He must have heard, for the flashlight beam swung round in her direction, horse and rider moving rapidly up the beach. She ran down to the channel's edge and then the light was full on her, blinding her. 'It may be too deep!' she yelled, indicating the water that lay between them.

'I'll give it a try,' he shouted back.

Rajah was a good two hands higher than Star, and far more powerfully built; even so, Stephen got wet to the knees in the deepest part of the channel. Joanna did not think she had ever seen a more welcome sight than the huge black stallion gaining a foothold on the sand. She was no longer alone. . . . Stephen leaned forward, his voice clipped with anger. 'Are you all right?' She nodded wordlessly. 'Can you get up behind me? We'd better cross right away, the tide's coming fast.'

By some kind of superhuman effort she flung herself across Rajah's back, putting her arms around Stephen's waist for support, and in a very cowardly manner closing her eyes as he urged Rajah back into the water. She could feel the bunching of the stallion's powerful muscles as he plunged into the current, then the chill waters were sucking at her boots, lapping round her knees. She held on tightly, and in a final lurch Rajah regained the beach.

The journey back was a nightmare, for her wet jodhpurs chafed Joanna's legs and her sweater was plastered to her skin as the rain continued to pour down. It was pitch dark. Stephen had turned off the flashlight, trusting to Rajah's eyes to guide them through the woods. Paying very little attention to where they were going, Joanna suddenly realised they were heading up the hill towards Stephen's house rather than across the fields to John's. She must have made some sound of protest, because he yelled back over his shoulder, 'It's closer—you're wet through!'

She didn't want to go to Stephen's. She wanted to go back to the farm, where Sally and John's presence would cushion her from Stephen's tamped-down anger. She rested her cheek against his back and closed her eyes, aware of her recurrent bouts of shivering almost as if they were happening to someone else. After that, things seemed to happen in a daze.

They stopped outside a commodious stone stable. By throwing his leg over Rajah's neck, Stephen slid to the ground; Joanna would have fallen had he not caught her. Without ceremony he lowered her to the ground under the eaves. 'Stay there,' he said tersely. 'I've got to put Rajah inside.'

She had no intention of moving, she decided fuzzily, resting her head on her knees. The next thing she knew she was being lifted as if she was a sack of grain, and carried up to the house, through the back door and the kitchen, down the long hallway to a room she had never been in before, obviously Stephen's bedroom. Stephen kicked open the door to an adjoining bathroom, sitting her in a wicker chair by the door. 'Start getting your clothes off,' he ordered. 'I'll phone John and let him know you're safe.'

'Star?' she queried, raising a white, anxious face.

'Arrived at John's just as I was about to go and look for you. There's no harm done to her—no thanks to you!'

As he went out of the room she was left with the memory of his grim, tight-lipped face, so that she shivered from more than the cold. Bending over, she tried to pull off her boots, but they were too wet and she had too little energy, and she soon gave up the struggle, sitting hunched over in the chair.

Stephen came back in, saying briefly, 'John's glad you're okay.'

'That's more than can be said for you,' she snapped.

He looked straight at her. 'I'm so damned angry with you, it's as much as I can do to keep my hands off you. Hold out your foot.' With no noticeable gentleness he hauled off her boots. Then he reached for her sweater.

She shrank back. 'I can manage

'Don't be silly—you'll catch your death of cold if you stay in those clothes any longer.' The sweater was tugged over her head, and then he had pulled her to her feet and was stripping the wet jodhpurs down over her hips.

Clad only in her underwear, a most inadequate covering, she said defiantly, 'You can turn on the shower and then you can leave. Please,' she added as an afterthought.

Stephen brushed past her, turning on the taps full strength and pulling a heap of fluffy towels out of the cupboard. The wallpaper was extremely attractive, she thought irrelevantly, as were the wicker accessories and the cascade of potted plants around the window. Then he said brusquely, 'I'll be outside if you need anything,' and mercifully closed the door behind him. Releasing her pent-up breath in a sigh of relief, Joanna adjusted the water temperature and stepped under the jet of steaming hot water.

She had never enjoyed a shower more in her life. The heat gradually penetrated her whole body, relaxing her muscles and calming her overstrained nerves. Not until she had lathered herself with soap and shampooed her hair did she step out on the mat, wrapping herself in one of the luxuriously soft towels and drying her hair on another. Only then did she realise that she had nothing to wear. A quick survey of the bathroom yielded no other possibilities than the voluminous bath towel. Holding on to it firmly, she opened the door. 'Stephen, do you have a robe I can . . .?'

Her voice died away, for he was standing no more than two feet away from her, taking a shirt from the top drawer of the bureau. He had taken off his own wet clothes, and was wearing only a pair of slim-fitting whipcord trousers, his chest and feet bare. Nervously she clutched the towel a little tighter.

'What happened to your face?' he demanded.

She touched her cheek lightly with her free hand. 'I scraped it on a rock on the island.'

'You little fool—you could have drowned, don't you realise that?'

She was no longer the drenched, shivering creature she had been twenty minutes ago. 'You're over-reacting,' she said coldly.

As he took a step closer, it took an actual effort of will for her not to retreat. 'Like hell,' he snapped roughly. 'How do you think I felt when I saw Star coming back without you in the middle of a storm at nightfall?'

The green eyes blazed at him. 'I have absolutely no idea how you feel about anything, Stephen Moore!'

He gripped her by the arm, his voice dangerously quiet. 'Well, you're about to find out. What the devil did you do it for, anyway—to give us all a scare?'

'Of course not!'

'Then why?'

Struck dumb, she stared at him in consternation. The towel slipped a fraction of an inch, and she didn't even notice. Though her brain whirled a kaleidoscope of pictures: the wild geese flying across the sky the first day she had met him; the sensitivity and fierce passion with which he had made love to her; the tension in his body when Laura had greeted him at Belle Maison, and the look in his eyes as he saw Karen for the first time in four years. . . . There was no point in trying to deceive him. She would be as honest with him as she knew how, and then as soon as she could she would request a transfer at the hospital and she would leave the Island.

She said quietly, 'I was in the barn when you were there with Karen ... I heard you tell her you loved her.'

His face gentled. The hand that had been clasped with punishing strength around her arm slid up to her shoulder and drew her closer to him. 'Why did that make you run away, Joanna?'

She stared at the dark, tangled hair on his chest, unable to meet his eyes. 'I—I didn't think I'd ever hear you say those words,' she stumbled miserably. 'I thought Laura had destroyed your ability to love. When I heard you say them to Karen—I was upset, that's all.'

He took her chin in his free hand. 'Look at me.'

Unwillingly she raised troubled green eyes, her heart skipping a beat as she saw the intent look on his face. 'I think she did destroy it for a while. I was afraid to get close to anyone ... but that's not true any more. And you're the main reason, Joanna—you, and Karen.'

Her throat was dry. 'I am?'

'Yes. Don't you understand why I was so angry with you tonight?' She shook her head. 'It's very simple—when I saw Star and thought something had happened to you, I nearly went out of my mind. Oh, Joanna, I've known for days, weeks, how much you mean to me, but there was always something holding me back, making me afraid of actually saying the words. But not any more.' He drew her closer so they were touching each other, body to body. 'Not any more ... I love you, Joanna. I love you. ...' His voice was exultant, his kiss as wild and powerful as the waves. Giving herself up to it, drowning in it, she put her arms around his neck, burying her fingers in his hair. The towel slipped further, and then he was loosening it so that it fell to the floor and his hands were all over her body and his kisses were raining on her mouth, her cheek, her throat.

'I want you so much—it seems like forever since that first time. . . .'

He carried her to the bed. She lay on her back, watching his eyes caress the curving lines of her body as he stripped off his clothes. Then he was with her, crushing her to him, his hands and mouth and body so urgent in his need of her that she opened to him as a flower does to the sun; in a burst of golden light the petals vanished, the barriers were broken and they became one.

She lay very still as the radiance slowly dimmed and reality reasserted itself. Stephen was heavy on her, and very warm, his heartbeat pounding against her breast. Filled with a happiness of which he was the source, she held him close, knowing with a certainty that would be with her until death that this was where she belonged; it was for this man that she had been born.

It was he who spoke first, laughter quivering in his chest. 'Sorry, sweetheart—I didn't mean to take you by storm like that.' He brought his hand up to her breast, cupping it very gently. 'It had been so long. Too long.' His voice suddenly deepened, the laughter gone from it. 'Oh, Joanna, I don't think I'll ever have enough of you! I love you so much.'

She was free to say it now, joyfully, endlessly free. 'I love you too, Stephen.'

He leaned up on one elbow, his hand still fondling her breast. 'You told me that before,' he said huskily. 'I wasn't ready for it then because I was still tied to the past, to all the conflicting memories of Laura.' He raised his head, looking past her into the dark shadows in the corner of the room. 'I needed those few days at Belle Maison. For four years I'd been caught in a dilemma I couldn't resolve: either something terrible had happened to Laura in the Caribbean and she was quite innocent of deception or wrongdoing, or she had schemed and plotted her escape, wilfully deceiving me and stealing my daughter from me. More and more it had begun to seem as though the latter was true. But I had no proof, so I was never quite able to believe she could have been so cruel.'

His face was the face of the Stephen she had first met, bitter and remote. Joanna said tentatively, 'You don't have to talk about it if you don't want to, Stephen. It's all right. . . .'

He glanced down at her. 'No, let me. Just once, and then we'll forget about it . . . when we went to Belle Maison and she was there, then I had my proof.' He laughed, a sound without humour. 'Oh, she tried her best to get out of it, used every trick in the book. But she soon found out they didn't work any more. I wasn't the same man I had been six or seven years ago. So then she started to bargain. She would give me legal custody of Karen in return for a certain amount of money—never mind how much. Plenty, you can be sure.'

Shocked to the core of her being, Joanna whispered, 'You mean she *sold* Karen to you?'

The grey eyes were bleak. 'That's what it amounted to. Karen, of course, must never know that. But that's why I had to stay longer than I'd anticipated. I certainly didn't want there to be any legal loopholes, so I went over all the documents with a fine toothcomb.'

She smiled ruefully. 'I won't tell you what *I* thought you were doing!'

His features relaxed as he smiled down at her. 'Not a chance!' Abruptly he sobered. 'When I look back, I can understand how it all happened. For all my academic achievements, I was almost totally inexperienced when I met Laura. I'd certainly never been in love before. I suppose I dumped on her all the emotion of twenty-seven years, building an idealised picture of her that was nowhere near the truth. Then when the picture began to crumble, I couldn't face it. If she was like that, then all women were like that. All women, that is, until you came along.' He grinned. 'Crashing into my life!'

'I did rather, didn't I?'

'You were different, Jo. Honest and straightforward, involved in life, not just on the sidelines as I'd felt I'd been for far too long. You *cared* about people. And you were so beautiful, with your big green eyes and your flame-red hair. A temper to match, I might add.'

'I haven't!'

He ruffled her hair. 'Yes, you have. Just so long as you know I'm the boss.'

She wrinkled her nose at him. 'Now that's debatable.'

'We'll have a long time to debate it—that is, you will marry me, won't you, Jo?'

'I've been wondering when you'd ask,' she said primly. Impulsively she reached up and kissed him. 'Yes, I'll marry you, Stephen.' She punctuated her words with kisses. 'Yes, yes, and yes!'

With unexpected humility he said, 'I don't deserve you, Jo.'

'Don't say that——'

'Tonight when I thought I might have lost you, I knew I'd been a fool not to have spoken to you sooner. But it was a shock finding Laura down there and finally realising what she was really like. For so long I'd thought my picture of her was the real picture, and it wasn't. I needed time, I think, to understand that the picture I had of you *was* the real one, that you *were* generous and sweet and true. And, of course, there was the whole new relationship with Karen.'

'That was why I was so upset this afternoon,' she confessed. 'You were able to tell Karen you loved her, but you'd never told me that.' She plucked at the bedspread. 'I was even jealous of her.'

'You have no need to be that, Joanna. I love you and trust you—you're my reality.'

Tears of sheer happiness shone in her eyes. 'As you are mine.'

'I can finally say this—that the past is closed, over and done with. I'm free of it.'

Her smile was brilliant, her words a pledge. 'And the future is ours.'

Stephen drew a hand slowly down the length of her body, watching the response shiver in her face. 'The present is ours, too. I must take you home to your brother. But first we could. . . .'

'Yes, we could, couldn't we?'

And this time they were in no hurry.